Unseen Senses

PETRA DONOVAN

First Edition 2024

Note from the Author

Like much of fiction, the book requires a suspension of disbelief. We often rely on visual descriptions to understand settings, characters, and emotions in writing. This book offered an opportunity to create a world where the other senses had to provide more context. As an author, it provided an amazing challenge.

However, it should be noted that blindness is a spectrum and not accurately depicted in the novel. Other considerations, like pressure, pain, and discomfort due to blindness, were also not covered. If this causes you concern or could be a trigger, please do not continue with the book.

I hope readers enjoy the characters, their unique personalities, their sensuality, and their strength in dealing with love, friendship, and family dynamics.

Chapter 1

Abigail Sorensen held back her thick hair with one hand while the other wafted the aroma of the cooking pot. She leaned in, breathing the scent and tasting the air on her tongue. As she tuned out the sounds of her apartment, she focused on the sizzle and pops of the sauteing onions. The pop noises had stopped, and only a light sizzle remained. She nodded her head in approval before continuing to the next step.

In a sightless world, where generations have been born and lived without the sense of sight, Abigail relied on her four senses to navigate her small corner of the world. The apartment kitchen was a refuge—a sanctuary that pulsated with the hum of life orchestrated by deft hands moving nimbly across countertops. The gentle ticking of the oven timer and the soft hum of the refrigerator provided a melodic backdrop, a rhythm of existence in a world woven with textures, scents, and sounds.

"Jules, reduce the stove heat to simmer. Please."

"Of course, Abigail. The heat on element one has been reduced to level three."

"Set the ambiance to Parisian Fall," she commanded, her voice cutting through the quiet with authority.

The room transformed as the artificial intelligence Jules tabulated and executed the choice. Soft chirps and leaves rustling enveloped the space while, as if in the distance, the accordion music of the Bal-musette played. The apartment felt transported to Paris. The atmosphere complimented the dinner for one she prepared.

Cooking was a source of comfort for her, but it also reminded her of her loneliness. No matter how many elaborate dinners or baked treats she made, they might never fill the void in her heart. Abigail chided herself for setting a Paris backdrop. A city of love would not help the melancholy funk.

As she moved through the routine, the echo of loneliness danced alongside her, growing louder with every slice and sizzle. Abigail longed for more. A connection, a thread to connect her heart to another. But her routine catered to one for a reason, and the unspoken desires would remain silent in a world that still had sound.

Abigail's stomach moaned as she maneuvered to the dining

table with a plate and bowl in hand. A thud and demanding meow interrupted before she started eating. "Venus, how nice of you to join me for dinner,' she said, ear-rubbing the demanded cat. "But you know onions are poisonous to cats, no matter how tantalizing it smells." Venus only responded with another indignant meow.

Teasing Venus, Abigail took an exaggerated spoonful of soup, taunting the pesky feline. "Do you think I would forget you?" Abigail said, responding to Venus's pawing at Abigail's hand. "I prepared something special for you tonight." She held out a small morsel of the baguette from the French onion soup. Abigail had soaked it in salmon oil as a special treat. Without hesitation, Venus snatched it with her teeth and dropped it on the table before eagerly licking and chewing. "You are such an uncivilized eater. Is this how all cats dine?" True to her nature, Venus ignored her and continued munching on the fishy morsel.

"Jules, is anything interesting in the news today?" She started their regular evening meal conversation.

"Yes, an announcement of improvement in haptic glove technology." Jules provided a recap on the topic that Abigail would find interesting. It reported that the enhancement will allow medical practitioners to use their hands for diagnosis instead of relying on the observations of an AI module.

"That is exciting," she said, pondering how to leverage the technology in other fields. It was one of the many marvels developed since the Sightless Plague.

After clearing her dishes, Abigail returned to the kitchen

to tidy up. Most of the cooking pots and utensils were destined for the dishwasher. She hand-washed her dishes and cutlery, part of her nightly practice. She turned on the water first, letting her ears gauge the pressure. While some people distinguish hot or cold water by sound, Abigail hadn't yet discerned the difference, but she tried every day. She let the water move over her hands and lace through her fingers, methodically washing each dish using a cloth and unscented dish soap, a perfect moment to let her mind wander.

Her dishwashing daydreams were interrupted by the trumpet fanfare of her mother's ringtone. "Hear ye, hear ye. Her Royal Matriarch, the Supreme Leader of the Sorensen's, is calling. Stand up straight and answer with respect!" Gwen Sorensen created the ringtone herself, believing it was appropriate for her station as the head of the family. It also reflected her style of humoring command. Abigail allowed the ringtone to remain, saving her energy for future battles. Battles with higher stakes. "Hello Mom, how are you this evening?" Abigail completed the dishes as her mother replied.

"Abigail, my dear. It feels like forever since we spoke." It has only been three days. "I have been sitting by the phone waiting for you to confirm your attendance at our anniversary celebration this weekend."

Abigail's attendance had never been optional. That meant there was an ulterior motive for her mother's call. The subject of the inquisition wasn't her attendance. The impetus of the call was to determine if she would bring a date. Feeling mischievous today, Abigail decided two could play a game of manipulation. "I'm not sure, Mom. I have lesson plans to create this weekend, and I was thinking of reorganizing my closets. Perhaps I will go to the pool."

"Stop that. You haven't been to the pool in at least a year. It is our fortieth wedding anniversary. Your absence would devastate your father." Playing the dad card, clever tactic, Abigail thought. While she loved her mother, it frustrated her that Gwen always had the upper hand in a game of wits.

While she spoke, Abigail moved through the apartment. She checked the windows and secured the door locks. An uncompromised evening routine. The apartment now secure, she flopped down on the sofa.

Abigail conceded to her mother, perhaps for self-preservation or a lack of will. She knew the family matriarch would soon start fake crying. It was hard to console tears of manipulation. "Of course I will be there. Do you need me to bring anything? I could make cookies?"

"No, my dear. I am having the celebration catered. Perhaps there is someone special you could bring? But not Tessa. I have already invited her."

Abigail mouthed a silent "crap". Her childhood friend usually served as her plus-one. Now Tessa was getting her own invite. "Mom, there is no one special, and I don't want to be grilled about it." Abigail couldn't avoid questions about marriage and starting a family. A well-meaning guest will suggest introducing her to someone they think would be perfect. Once Abigail could no longer handle the judgment, she would hide in her childhood bedroom closet. No one ever checks the closets looking for her.

"Mom, I could never bring someone to such an important celebration. Me showing up with someone after all this time would steal the spotlight from your special day." Confident in her resourcefulness, Abigail smiled, knowing her answer would deter her mother's persistence. Abigail absentmindedly began petting the cat that had hopped onto the sofa. Venus nestled onto her lap and emitted a soothing purr. Both were content with their successful manipulation.

"Oh, yes, I wouldn't want to put that type of pressure on you. I won't be able to control your aunties, but I will do my best." Ugh, the aunties. Most of those ladies were not biological aunts, but their close friendship granted them the title. "They all want to see you happy. It comes from a good place."

"I know. They all mean well." By 'all' Abigail was looping her mother into that category. "It would be nice if my happiness wasn't dependent on a man or a baby." Was this the hundredth time she had said those exact words? Was there a prize for repeating it so often?

"Yes, of course, dear. You can find happiness without a man or a baby." Dismissing the topic further, Gwen Sorensen continued, "I was hoping you could keep Tessa under control at the party. I love that girl like another daughter, but I can't have her misbehaving with the guests or the staff."

Abigail sputtered out a laugh, unable to hold it back. The truth was out. Today's call had nothing to do with Abigail coming to the party or a date. It was about putting a leash on Tessa. Her mother's concerns were valid, but the request would be equivalent to asking Abigail to hold back the water if it rained that day. Tessa was a force of nature.

"There is nothing wrong with Tessa's behavior, Mom. Perhaps you should ask your guests to control themselves around her." Abigail and Tessa were best friends. While she wanted to defend that friendship, she also needed to take pity on her mother. "I will do my best to keep Tessa entertained."

"Perfect, my dear, that is all I ask. I should continue making my calls. See you this weekend." The call disconnected.

"Okay Mom, love you. Say hi to Dad for me," Abigail said to the disconnected line. Talking to her mother felt like a whirlwind had gone through her head. She couldn't help feeling played from the moment the telephone proclaimed her mother's call. Had she ever had the upper hand?

Like most of their interactions, her mother's call reminded Abigail of what she felt was missing from her life. Abigail's life would be easier if she could deny her yearning for a partner. Someone to celebrate anniversaries and milestone with. She also longed to hold a baby of her own. She wanted those things. But she was terrified to trust anyone and let down her defensive walls.

Abigail had considered adoption; she could open her heart to a child, but that felt incomplete. She knew single parenting was possible, but couldn't abandon the partner-shaped void. Abigail considered her parents to be her goal, with a little less manipulation of her children. Abigail wanted someone to partner with. Someone whose strengths and weaknesses offset her own.

A single tear slid down Abigail's cheek as she mourned for her old life. For the last five years, she had considered her existence in terms of pre- and post-attack.

Pre-attack, Abigail not only dated but thought she had found the one. She had played the field and imagined futures with every eligible and at least one ineligible man she met. But meeting Ryker had fit in her vision for her future—their future.

Post-attack, Abigail avoided interactions, mentally constructing walls and moats to keep people at a safe distance. She also learned that Ryker was the sort of man who jumped ship when times were tough. Abigail rubbed her neck, recalling the welts from where her purse strap had been used to choke her. The botched purse snatching had resulted in weeks of physical recovery and now years of emotional trauma.

Abigail gave herself a shake and cleared her throat. She could not dwell on it much longer without her anxiety getting out of control. After rechecking the locks, she headed to bed. Alone.

In the embrace of the weighted blanket, Abigail felt the comforting presence pressing her into the mattress—a tangible reminder of past loves and the shared intimacies of a bed. However, these memories, though vivid, lacked the warmth of human touch, and no cozy blanket could replace the comforting embrace of a partner's arms.

Tracing the tips of her fingers across her face, Abigail allowed herself to imagine sensations if it had not been her touch. These imaginary caresses, filled with tenderness and longing, teased her into yearning for something more profound. Despite this desire, a persistent fear held her back, making her hesitant to open herself to vulnerability.

The longing intensified, and she ached to place her hands on someone's chest and feel the reassuring thud of their heartbeat. Yet, the fear of potential heartache and disappointment lingered, creating a barrier that kept her from pursuing the desired connection.

With each deliberate breath, she tried to control the slow release of her apprehensions. In the quiet room, she discerned only her scent, a solitary presence in a space that had long awaited the warmth of shared moments. Another's breath absent and the untouched side of the bed. Isolation weighed on her unwelcome companion.

Sensing Abigail's solitude, Venus thudded against the mattress and kneaded the bedding, creating her cozy space. Curling into a protective ball, the cat fell asleep, her purrs providing a gentle backdrop to Abigail's contemplations.

As the embrace of sleep enveloped Abigail, she grappled with a profound question—whether she could rediscover the original Abigail, who approached life with unbridled enthusiasm. If the answer came, it was lost in the last few minutes of consciousness before sleep finally overtook her.

Chapter 2

Jules instructed Abigail to veer right to avoid a pedestrian. Instead, she veered left and clipped her foot and shin on a stone step. The lack of sleep from the night before had left her feeling sluggish and unable to concentrate. Abigail let out a curse, her words echoing through the air, and then apologized to her surroundings, mindful of any nearby children. It might have been safer to stay in bed, but duty called, and she had to go to school.

Abigail was already running late as she bumbled through the coffee shop's door. The rich aroma of brewing coffee enveloped her as she navigated to their usual table. The gurgles, steam, and pops of the coffee machine were like an auditory map of the café. Even Jules had gone quiet, its watchful presence not needed in the familiar territory.

She couldn't start the workday without meeting her best friend for an aromatic tea or coffee. As a high school biology teacher, she needed that burst of caffeine and lighthearted conversation with Tessa, an English instructor at the same school.

"Mornin. Already ordered your tea," Tessa's sleepy voice slurred. Abigail wasn't alone in starting the day on the wrong note. But at least Tessa was running on time.

Abigail's acute sense of smell caught a hint of alcohol lingering in the air, intermingling with freshly toasted bagels. Tessa's movements were sluggish, and the sounds of her gulping down coffee revealed an underlying discomfort that Abigail could almost touch.

"Tess, are you hung over?" Abigail sat opposite Tessa, careful not to spill the tea.

"I don't know, Mom, am I?" Tessa responded, gulping down coffee loud enough for the entire café to hear.

"Sarcasm noted, I'll take that as an affirmative on being inebriated. We partied hard on a Thursday night, did we?" Abigail's shoulders slumped as she rubbed her temples. "It seems like it is every few days. Maybe mothering is what you need," Abigail reprimanded.

Unfazed, Tessa tore off a chunk of her bagel and shoved it into her mouth. Still chewing, she replied, "It was a 'we' situation, was it? I don't recall you being there. However, we are still young. We should be living it up. There was a time you would have been out all night with me, a walk of pride straight to school. Don't judge." Tessa ripped another piece of bagel, smacking her lips together like an insulant child as she chewed.

Tessa's words landed with the impact of sharp fingernails on Abigail's face. A wince played on her features, laying bare the depth of her emotional turmoil. It was one thing for Abigail to regret the loss of the old her, but it hurt more to have Tess shove it back in her face. "Not nice, Tessa Sato. You're judging me. I am worried about you. How are you going to manage teaching this morning? You are going to get fired."

Tessa stuck out her tongue and blew raspberries in Abigail's direction. "A coffee now, a bagel to reset the tummy, and I will fill a thermos of coffee before we leave. The first period can draft some crappy poem about spring."

"Solid plan. Don't forget to add water and perhaps a banana." Despite the childish behavior, Abigail still offered wisdom, albeit delivered in an annoyed tone. Tessa wasn't wrong that Abigail once had a wild side that needed quick cures.

Tessa mumbled something close to 'meh', perhaps a maybe-yes combo. "Thanks, Abi. I shouldn't have been so snarky." While not a complete apology, Tessa's acknowledgment was still a big deal. Silence fell between them, letting a few seconds of café noise reset their conversation.

The exotic scent of orange, ginger, and basil stirred the senses as Abigail raised her teacup. "Did Jules message you I was in an orange mood this morning?"

"Nope, I just know you that well. Yesterday was berries, so there was a good chance today would be citrus or chai."

"I will have to shake up my routine a bit. My predictability has become predictable," Abigail mused out loud. "Speaking of shaking things up, how was your evening?" Abigail asked, trying to open the conversation with no judgment this time.

"Good, I was out with Terrance." Tessa's curt response reeked of faux innocence.

"The Terrance, as in third-date-in-a-row Terrance?" Abigail could not hide her shock. Second dates were rare, but three were unheard of.

"Last date, Terrance, I figured one more night out before I let him down easy," Tessa explained. "We both got something out of our time together, but he's a nice guy, and I could see myself falling for someone like him." Abigail shook her head; when Tessa saw the potential to find happiness with one person, she was determined to undermine it.

"Would that be so bad? Find someone you like and continue to enjoy your time together." Abigail challenged.

"Not in my immediate future. I want it easy. No shared spaces, no shared possessions, no commitments." Tessa repeated this mantra several times over the last decade of their friendship.

"I wish more for you."

"And I wish my best friend would leave the safety of her apartment and let her wild side out to play," countered Tessa, smashing her mug to the table's surface. Tessa's hands flew to her mouth, slapping at her face as if trying to scoop her words up and shove them back in. "Oh my god, Abi. I am so sorry. I shouldn't have said that." Tessa reached out to find Abigail's hand, which Abigail recoiled as if the touch burned her.

Abigail put her tea down and sat back in her chair. "Wow, tell me how you feel," her caustic, pained voice said.

Tessa sputtered the beginning of a few replies, trying to reverse what she had done. Finally, shaking her head as if settling an internal argument, Tess decided on the truth. "Every day, I dance around the unsaid. You are one of the most important people in my world. You're second only to my mom, but you're like a ghost of the vibrant woman I knew. It hurts to see you this way." Tessa paused, but when Abigail didn't respond, she continued, "I damaged my verbal filter this morning because I said it all wrong. But it needed to be said. You deserve to find 'someone'. That won't happen secluded in your tower with a cat and an AI."

"That's not fair. I leave my apartment, and you know why I don't trust people." Abigail pouted, crossing her arms across her chest to strengthen her internal resolve.

"You leave for work, sometimes for dinner with either Imani or me, and perhaps to get groceries. But even then, you try to have it auto-delivered. Abigail, someone took something from you, and you have never tried taking it back. I can't fathom your struggle, but I know the pain of seeing a friend change. You're merely a shell of your former self." Tessa sniffled and wiped the tears which were now trickling down her cheek.

Her throat muscles tightened, and Abigail felt the tension of unexpressed sorrow. Emotional pain constricted her ability to breathe and swallow, much like the physical pain had that night. The café's sound felt hollow, drowned out by the whine echoing in her ears. How could she communicate her longing to reclaim her former identity? She picks up her phone almost every night, wanting to call and suggest something crazy and reckless. It wasn't just the fear of being hurt again holding her back. She feared failing herself, her old self. Abigail gave herself a small shake, willing the thoughts of that night to retreat.

Moments passed between the two women. A combination of monosyllabic sounds came from them both. Neither knew what should be said next. Abigail forced her throat to swallow, willed her muscles to release, and broke the silence, "Some days, I miss her too," the words choked out, tears pooling in her eyes. Abigail returned her hand to the table, reaching out to find Tessa's hand to grip. The thoughts of the previous night and now Tessa's unexpected revelation had unraveled the carefully woven threads of Abigail's composure.

"Abi, I am so sorry." Tessa gushed out.

Abigail patted Tessa's hand. "I know you are." With her untamed spirit and unyielding honesty, Tessa had been Abigail's steadfast anchor for years. In every laughter shared and every wild escapade embraced, she stood as a poignant reminder of the carefree soul Abigail used to be. Every word Tessa spoke, including the apology, was sincere.

Abigail's chest tightened as she expelled a long breath, a futile attempt to regain control of the emotional turmoil that threatened to consume her. Already vulnerable from the prior night's reflections, the echoes of the intense conversation reverberated in her mind, leaving her feeling emotionally exposed, like a raw nerve laid bare.

"Well, not how I expected the morning to go. We should pull ourselves together and head to school." Abigail drank back what remained of her tea, the ceramic warmth grounding her amid the emotional storm.

Tessa's agreement was evident in her subtle posture shift as she prepared to leave the table. Before standing, she firmly stated, "We must leave, Abigail, but our conversation isn't over," steadying the emotional sea with her voice.

"I know," Abigail replied, her head turning away from Tessa. The weight of unspoken words lingered in the air, a silent agreement that the depth of their discussion demanded more time.

The café hummed around them, oblivious to the emotional unraveling between the two friends. Abigail's fingers traced the rim of her empty teacup, seeking comfort in its familiar contours. The residue of vulnerability clung to the air like an unseen mist.

Tessa's following words carried a mixture of resolve and concern. "Abigail, I want you to know I care about you. Whatever you're going through, you don't have to face it alone."

Abigail's throat tightened again, the dam straining to burst again. The sincerity in Tessa's words hit her with force. She turned her head back towards Tessa, trying to project the gratitude she couldn't articulate in words. At that moment, amidst the unspoken pain and the weight of shared history, Abigail felt a glimmer of connection—a lifeline in the tumultuous sea of her emotions.

The café noise seemed to soften, and together, they gathered their belongings, preparing to face the day that awaited them outside the comforting walls of the café.

Chapter 3

As Abigail and Tessa arrived at the school, the hallways were a hive of frantic scurrying. They parted ways and were swept into the currents flowing through the corridors.

Abigail clicked on her earpiece and activated Jules again, now that she was at school.

"Remember, today you have that meeting after the third period," Jules reminded her, its voice more formal and efficient for the school environment.

"Wouldn't dream of missing it." Abigail slipped into her role as Ms. Sorensen, the high school biology teacher who navigated through her world with a grace that served her sightless society.

While the haptic devices would help most people, including Abigail, navigate the halls of the educational institute, Abigail preferred using the tactile lines embossed along the walls. The groves were the scars from early navigation methods. A line etched in the walls' surface that a person could use a finger or hand to guide them, little markers on position, and potential offshoots to other walls and hallways. Abigail's fingers traced the lines etched on the walls, each groove a testament to the collective journey of countless hands. The walls, once etched by primitive navigation, now hummed with the gentle vibrations of technological progress. The tactile connection symbolized physical guidance and shared history, a harmony of past and present.

When she reached her classroom, Abigail could feel the vitality of her first-period students pulsating out into the hall. Most were fifteen or sixteen years old, and their voices mingled in conversation and laughter. They deserved her best, despite the rocky start to her day.

As Abigail shuffled through her teaching materials, her fingers traced the familiar grooves of the embossed label for the first period. Each touch paired with a connection to her well-worn routine.

As the chatter fell silent, a symphony of anticipation enveloped the room. Abigail, attuned to the subtle shifts in sound, could discern the chorus of AI companions whispering in her students' ears. The air hummed with the collaborative dance of human curiosity and artificial intelligence, creating a multi-sensory prelude to the lesson. It was like having a teacher's assistant assigned to each student. Abigail just needed to ensure they were all getting the same message. "Everyone, please calibrate companions to the class AI so we can begin."

"Today, we are going to review genetics and the Mendelian square. Place your hands on the braille diagrams before you so we can begin." Abigail, or rather Ms. Sorensen, began the lesson.

"Love is sparking at the back of the class, I see," Jules murmured into Abigail's earpiece, discreet as ever.

"Is it now?" Abigail mused, tipping her head towards the back to see if love would lead to disruption. Without sight, teachers had to rely on integrating AI to alert them to anything they should be concerned about. But Abigail was selective of where she would intervene, and if it was innocent, consensual, and did not disrupt learning, she turned a literal blind eye. It was a tender echo of her youthful fumbling and clumsy attempts to touch every moment.

"We will let it be," Abigail whispered to Jules and continued the lesson.

Abigail tried to leave five to ten minutes at the end of each class for questions and answers on any biology-related topic. She prided herself on open dialogue and creating safe spaces. During the second period, her earpiece advised Pedro had a question. "Pedro, what would you like to talk about?"

Pedro was quiet a moment and whispered, 'The Sightless Plague'. Abigail could hear him shifting in his chair and assumed it was with unease.

"Okay, Pedro," Abigail said, her voice warm and encouraging. "'The Sightless Plague' is always an interesting topic. What are you curious about?" She complimented the topic and hoped to give Pedro more confidence.

"It is hard to articulate. I wonder why we are still here instead of being wiped out?" Pedro's voice wobbled with emotions he was trying to hold back. Adolescence is hard, and it is not unusual to question our reason for being even before the plague.

"Despite what some of you may think," Abigail chuckled at her upcoming joke, "I am not as ancient as the dinosaurs, so I wasn't around during the plague, but I can offer my opinion." A small laugh escaped some students as Abigail used self-deprecation to lighten the mood. One of many tools in her teaching arsenal.

"Who can provide a brief recap of how the plague happened?" Abigail encouraged group participation.

"An innocuous retrovirus that resulted in mild flu-like systems for the host. Unbeknownst to the scientist, the virus reproduced and hijacked reproductive cells, resulting in a mutation for future generations." Augusto supplied a concise description.

"Well said, very clinical language, Augusto. This process has happened before in the history of life, including our distant ancestors. This transfer of genetic material has even helped animal species. Anything I can clarify before I move on to Pedro's question?" Abigail waited a moment, not surprised there at the lack of questions. Most of them already had a basic, if not in-depth, understanding of the plague science.

"I assume the question is less about the actual science and more about the behavior that allowed us to survive. I cannot pretend to comprehend the impact this would have had on our ancestors. But humans did what they always do: find a way. At first, science focused on a cure. Still, after years without progress, the scientific community shifted from cure to building the infrastructure to allow the next generations to live." Abigail paused for dramatic effect.

"We don't always get things right, but when those with sight combined their efforts with those without, a significant leap forward occurred in the technology infrastructure we use today. Educators taught new generations how to continue progressing in their new world."

"We're here because we, as a species, never gave up. Despite our survival, there was a sizable decrease in the population. Some individuals and governments gave up or ignored the issue until it was too late to recover. But you, Pedro, and everyone else in this room are the descendants of those who did not give up. That survival grit is now part of our DNA, or at least our psyche, and that is why you are here today. Does my response answer your question?"

"I think so, Ms. Sorensen."

"Wonderful." While she took a certain amount of creative license, Abigail loved providing the inspirational speech, even if she didn't feel her ancestorial grit pulsing in her veins anymore.

Abigail entered the faculty lounge for lunch, feeling drained. An evening with restless sleep, and emotional morning tea, and now two periods of teaching had left her spent.

Aside from the Sightless Plague question, the second period had been uneventful. While she could talk about the plague and its cascading impact for hours, Tessa would not want that conversation. Abigail opted to share the budding romance from the first period with Tessa. "They are probably so proud they got away with it," Abigail smiled while shaking her head.

"Remember your first serious crush, Abigail?" she asked between mouthfuls of her lunch.

"Vividly," Abigail admitted, the corners of her lips curling upwards. "I remember thinking his voice sounded like chocolate tastes—rich and smooth."

"Sounds delicious," Tessa chuckled.

"Oh, he was scrumptious." Abigail sighed, remembering how she got to taste every part of him.

"Time to discover more than a tasty voice for you. Perhaps a full sensory package." While the words seemed innocent, Tessa's suggestion sounded sensual and verged on naughty for the teachers' lounge.

"Tessa, stop. You are making me blush," Abigail said, dropping her voice to a whisper, wondering who might be listening, a human or an AI.

"No one will know you are blushing unless they touch

your face, which might be interesting."

"Tessa, you are like a rabid dog with meaty bison bone."

Tessa continued, as if she hadn't understood a word of Abigail's discomfort. "Girl, I get it. You want the full package—the touch, the taste, the laughter... and maybe even the awkwardness of two people figuring out how to fit together," Tessa said, her words a blend of humor and earnestness. "And trust me, there's plenty of awkwardness."

"Tell me about it," Abigail laughed, the sound mingling with the symphony of dishes moving at once in the faculty lounge. "But I guess it's the thrill of the unknown, the uncertainty that makes it all worthwhile."

"Exactly!" Tessa exclaimed. "Are you prepared to leap once more? To dive into the messy, wonderful world of dating?"

Aghast, Abigail responded, "Uh, who said I was diving into dating?"

"The longing in your voice since you sat down at this table and started talking about fifteen-year-olds falling in love,' Tessa responded sternly. "You cannot live vicariously through your students. It's just wrong on multiple levels. It's time to saddle up and get back on a horse or a herd." She used her no-bullshit-call-it-as-it-is tone. There was no escaping her now.

Abigail didn't know how to respond. She knew Tessa was accurate, though not entirely about a herd of horses, but she was correct about getting out there. Admitting it was the hard part.

Abigail's lack of response encouraged Tessa to proclaim,

"We're putting Operation Love Quest into action."

"Operation what now?" Abigail asked, confused and suspicious.

"Hey, every glorious mission needs a name. And your mission, my dear Abigail, is about to begin." Tessa's playful tone promised a response that Abigail was unsure how to respond to.

"Tonight, your place. I will even concede and invite Imani. We will bring a few bottles of wine. You will cook dinner. We will hash out the plan sometime while eating and drinking." Tessa's instructions allowed for no compromise.

Abigail replayed Tessa's words, ensuring she knew what she agreed to. "Okay?" Abigail responded. At least she would have company tonight and she would make dinner so tasty they would not even think about Operation Love Quest.

The aroma of sizzling garlic wafted through Abigail's kitchen. Its tendrils wrapped around Tessa like a comforting embrace, luring her like a moth to a flame. As Abigail stirred the pot, her hands danced with practiced grace, each movement a testament to a life elegantly adapted to darkness.

"It smells like heaven in here, Abi," Tessa announced as she entered the room, her voice a symphony of cheer and mischief that echoed through the kitchen. "You should think about becoming a chef."

"Nope, not thick-skinned enough to take the judgment.

But I have thought about judging others."

"As in judging competitions? Sign me up for that too."

"As in food critic. Maybe on a food blog where I can share my recipes or improve bad dishes from famous restaurants." Heat rushed to Abigail's cheeks. She had never shared this dream with anyone before, not even Jules. Why had she never told Tessa? She wondered. This wasn't a whim. Something previously prevented her from speaking the want. She had censored herself.

"You would be great at that. You wouldn't even have to leave your teaching job. So, the question on everyone's mind, Ms. Sorensen, why haven't you done it yet?"

Instead of sharing that she was a chickenshit, Abigail changed the conversation, "Imani called. She won't make it tonight. Poor thing is tied up at the lab."

"Tied up at a lab sounds kinky," Tessa said, grabbing wine glasses from the cabinet. "But Miss Goody-Goody Ice Princess is not likely to be tied up that way."

"Tessa, that's not nice. Imani is not an Ice Princess or a goody-goody. She has so much pressure on her." Abigail added fresh herbs to the pot. "As a consolation for missing tonight, she says she can meet us tomorrow night at La Karnali."

"La-de-da, how upscale. We can put off plotting your love quest until tomorrow. I get you and all this food to myself," Tessa said, handing Abigail a glass of wine.

"Tess, I—"

"Abigail Sorensen," Tessa interjected, feigning exasperation as she plucked a spoon from the drawer and dipped it into the simmering sauce. "When will you stop feeding others and start feeding your desires? You know, the spicy kind? My GOD, this is good!" Tessa double-dipped another spoonful.

Abigail exhaled long, trying to overcome the discomfort this conversation was causing. Tessa's audacity could be as overwhelming as her perfume, a floral assault that signified her arrival long before words were exchanged. "I'm not exactly starving, Tess."

"Please share when you last went on a date. Your definition of intimate touch is bumping elbows with Mr. Simmons in the faculty lounge."

"Which is always thrilling," Abigail deadpanned, earning a chuckle from Tessa. Mr. Simmons, Tyler, was a wonderful man, probably one of the nicest men in the faculty, but he didn't get Abigail's heart racing. He was timid and seemed even less at ease than Abigail. Despite being the same age, Tyler felt like a younger brother who needed protection, not a love interest.

"Seriously though, don't you crave that connection? That electric shock when someone's hand brushes against yours, or the warmth that floods you when lips meet just the right way?"

Abigail paused, the spoon hovering above the pot as Tessa's words conjured memories of tentative fingers intertwining, of breaths mingling with hesitant whispers. She remembered the flutter of eyelashes against her cheek, the taste of a kiss that echoed through the years.

"Of course I do," Abigail murmured, resuming her stirring with more force than necessary. "But it's not that simple, Tess."

"You've got more guts than anyone I know. It's high time you put yourself out there. Let yourself feel, Abi."

"Feel?" Abigail shook her head, her body disagreeing with Tessa before her mouth could. 'I feel too much." Abigail whipped in a wide circle, sending some sauce flying. She will need Jules to point out what Venus doesn't clean up.

"You are feeling the wrong things." Tess placed her hand over Abigail's, steadying her. Tessa shifted gears. "New plan: we will go out to dinner tomorrow at the bougie restaurant. We act uncivilized, let our hair down, and have fun. Let's see if a little exposure to fun renews you."

"Act uncivilized? You terrify me sometimes, Tess."

Chapter 4

The evening's debauchery began at Karnali, the upscale restaurant that promised its clients a euphoric sensory experience. Abigail, Tessa, and Imani walked through the double doors together, eager to discover Karnali's carnal reputation. As they entered, the room was filled with the captivating sounds of sultry instrumental music, its notes intertwining and caressing the air like delicate strands of silk. As the soft melody filled the air, hushed whispers and tinkling silverware dissipated, giving way to a subdued buzz of contentment among the patrons.

The air was thick with an alluring aroma that seemed to wrap around Abigail like a warm embrace, pulling her in with its seductive notes. The atmosphere was hushed and intimate, creating a sense of privacy that made her feel almost daring. She couldn't help but feel that this was no ordinary evening, and she was eager and nervous to explore what lay ahead.

A smooth voice welcomed them to Karnali and escorted them through the dining room with ease. With each table they passed, different delectable notes tickled Abigail's senses. She couldn't imagine how the taste of the food could surpass the aroma.

They nestled into a plush booth. The velvet cushions cradled them, and Abigail could not help but rub her hand back and forth against the short fibers. The texture provided comfort, like stroking a pet or running your hands across a newly buzzed head. A server took their drink orders and handed them the braille menu.

"Have you read this menu?" Tessa exclaimed, her voice a mix of awe and amusement. "It's meant to engage all our senses–taste, sound, smell, and touch. How deliciously decadent!"

Imani chuckled. "I've heard remarkable things about this establishment. They say it's an experience unlike any other."

Abigail hesitated, feeling out of her comfort zone before admitting, "It sounds exciting, though I'm a little nervous. This isn't my cooking."

"Embrace the adventure, Abigail!" Tessa enthused. "This isn't about your cooking, as good as it is. Pretend you are a food critic. No, don't pretend. Be a food critic, even if you don't write a detailed review."

"Okay, I can do that." Abigail nodded her head to herself. She would do this.

As they perused the menu, the scents of various dishes

wafted toward them, teasing their senses and making their mouths water. The sound of the ingredients being prepared in the open kitchen blended with the aroma of spices, creating a sensory tapestry that piqued their curiosity.

"Listen to that sizzle," Imani murmured appreciatively, directing their attention to the sound of something delectable cooking nearby.

"Maybe we should order one of everything," Tessa suggested, only half-joking.

Abigail couldn't help but smile at her friend's enthusiasm, feeling the excitement bubble inside her. "All right," she conceded, "let's indulge our senses and see where this evening takes us."

They did not order for everything on the menu, but opted for a tasting menu guaranteed to 'awaken the senses'. When their drinks arrived, they settled into cheery conversation while waiting to indulge in the culinary experience.

"Speaking of indulging our senses," Imani mused, "you know how stereotypes from before the plague? Men as tall, dark, and handsome, women as bombshell blondes?"

Abigail and Tessa burst into laughter before Imani could finish her thought. "It's so bizarre!" Abigail exclaimed. "I can't even relate to those descriptions. What might a bombshell blonde be referencing? I can only think of something explosive."

"Right? Weirdly, I can ask an AI my hair color, but it has no value." Tessa agreed, ruffling her hair. "But a smooth scalp to trace or thick hair to bury your fingers in? Now that makes sense!"

"Absolutely," Imani chimed in, regaining control of the conversation. "And it got me thinking about what we find attractive in a partner based on our senses. For example, I like earthy smells, like leaves in the autumn, and cedar trees. The feeling of a soft body with enough padding that I don't feel like I am lying next to a sheet of steel." Imani's voice went low and her pace slowed as if she each word was a sudden revelation. "I need to be with someone who is a direct contrast to the sterile, cold, lifeless environment of my research lab." Imani's voice tapered off with a note of sadness. Abigail suspected Imani's realization and her need for reflection.

Tessa did not seem to notice Imani's emotional state; if she did, she didn't care. Tessa blurted out, "I love men who smell like rain—clean rain, not worms and mud." Not that Abigail or Imani would have thought Tessa was talking about mud or worms. Well, maybe the mud—it has an earthy quality Imani enjoyed. "And kissing someone whose mouth tastes cool like vanilla ice cream gives me shivers." She paused, sipping her drink, lingering on the sensation. "Oh, and speaking of hair, I like long, at least long enough to wrap around my fingers. Can't say why it just feels intoxicating." Tessa seemed oblivious to the monopolization of the conversation and over sharing.

"Interesting," Abigail mused, reflecting on her preferences. "I am unsure about hat attracts my senses. Something with an exotic and spicy flavor, like the dishes I cook? I never thought about it. It's possible that what I really need is the complete opposite."

"Maybe you need to sample from the buffet and figure it out," Tessa teased.

"You are incorrigible, Tessa Sato," Abigail retorted, laughing with her friend.

Abigail reflected on Imani's early tone and wanted to shift the conversation away from herself. A brilliant scientist, Imani had dedicated her life to researching regaining sight. However, despite her determination, the demanding hours and seclusion must have affected her.

In a conversation lull, Abigail's curiosity prevailed. "Imani, or should I say, Dr. Larson," she said with mock formality to lighten the mood before she continued with her question, " I hope I'm not being too nosy...how is your research going?"

Imani exhaled a sigh of disappointment and leaned back in the booth with exhaustion. "To be honest, it's frustrating. There has been little progress on my end, or anyone else's, for that matter. After generations of living in a world without sight, people are questioning what it would mean to regain it."

"Really?" Abigail asked, genuinely surprised. "I've always found the idea of seeing and experiencing the world in a new way fascinating."

"Some people feel that way," Imani acknowledged. "But our population doesn't miss something they never had. Sight would be more like giving the entire population a superpower they may be unable to manage. There is also fear—fear of the unknown, the potential upheaval that restoring sight might bring if it were not inclusive to everyone. As a result, public funding for sight recovery projects is becoming sparse. I worry that one day I won't be able to continue my research."

"Could you get private funding to continue?" Tessa asked. Abigail was surprised that Tessa showed interest in Imani's work without mocking her.

"I will never take part in privately funded research," Imani responded with revulsion. "The private funding comes from parties that do not want equality. It would give a superpower to a select few for their gain. It is a terrifying prospect." Abigail could sense Imani's disdain. It was as if each word was punctuated with sourness tainting her mouth.

"Okay, no sighted overlords ruling the planet. Good plan." Despite Tessa's comedic delivery, the prospect frightened them all. Abigail, like most, wondered about life with sight but overlooked the risks. Sight was a novelty, as if humans were born with tails. An enjoyable past trait, offering new interactions with surroundings.

Abigail frowned, feeling a pang of sympathy for her friend. "That must be incredibly disheartening, especially given how passionate you are about your work."

Imani's voice softened. "It can be, yes. But I'm not passionate about my research because I think society would be better with sight or because I'm dissatisfied with being unable to see. It's just..." She paused, struggling to find the right words. "The Sightless Plague is a puzzle that has stumped generations, and I want to prove myself by solving it. I want to leave my mark on society."

Abigail nodded, understanding the drive behind Imani's passion. She extended her hand, her fingers grazing against Imani's. "I know you'll make a difference, Imani," she said earnestly. "You're one of the most determined people I've ever met, and if anyone can crack this puzzle, it's you."

"Thank you, Abigail," Imani replied, her voice touched with emotion. "Your support means more to me than you know."

Quiet fell between the three friends, the mood shifting after Imani shared her update. "I'm sorry, you two. We are supposed to be having a fun night out, scheming about Abigail's love life, and I've turned it into a lecture on my work. I am sorry to ruin the mood." Imani chastised herself.

"You didn't ruin the mood," Abigail said. "How often do we get such an exclusive insight into the brilliant mind of Dr. Imani Larson? If anything, it makes our night out even more special."

"Sure, special. But perhaps we make that our only depressing topic for the evening. I want to take this evening on more of a debauchery direction than evolutionary sciences." Tessa said.

Their food arrived that moment, interrupting Imani's need to continue apologizing. "Dinner is here. I can't wait to try it."

With eager anticipation, Abigail selected an amuse-bouche, her stomach grumbling its impatience while her mouth already salivated. The rectangle morsel was both firm and soft between her fingers. It held its shape, but Abigail knew the structure would give way if she pushed with her fingers. She first raised the sample to her nose. There was something peppery that made her nose twitch with a tickle. The smell of cilantro was pleasant and comforting. Her shoulders relaxed. Abigail touched the food to her lips, waking her taste buds in anticipation. It was cool against her skin, with a glossy smooth finish. She placed the bite in her mouth, closing it before letting her teeth pierce the exterior wall. Abigail grabbed for the table as an intense rush of flavors overpowered her. Pearls of lime popped with each movement of her teeth, bathing her palate with citrus and a mellow cream. "That, that was..." Abigail trailed off, unable to find the right word.

"Orgasmic," Tessa supplied, breathless.

"Yes, I believe that is the only way to describe it," Abigail agreed, releasing her grip on the table and trying to recover. "Perhaps you should become the food critic."

"That may have been too indulgent for me. I feel a little overwhelmed, maybe even lightheaded. I hope not every taste is so intense." Imani said, collapsing back in her seat. "I mean, it was good. Just a lot for one little piece of food. The body can only handle so much."

"Well, I can handle a lot more. I don't believe I have ever had something that good in my mouth." Tessa snickered at her joke. "Perhaps we should have asked the server for something from the kid's menu for Imani." Abigail winced at Tessa's insult.

"If you are going to act like a child, Tessa, we should get a kid's menu for you instead." Abigail retorted. Abigail hated Tessa's jabs at Imani. Despite Tessa's confident facade, Abigail was aware of her underlying insecurities. Unfortunately for Imani, she embodied two of them. Tessa was afraid of looking like a fool and was terrified that Abigail would one day value Imani's friendship over hers.

Imani interjected, trying to diffuse the growing tension. "Ladies, let's not let one bite of food sabotage our evening. It was a good bite of food, but hardly worth stooping to insults and food fights."

"That would be a terrible waste of food." Tessa's acknowledgment was as close to an apology as she could offer. Abigail made a note to talk to Tessa about the tension later.

"If that was just the first sample, I can't imagine what the rest of the menu would be like." Abigail traced her bottom lip, reigniting her mouth's response to the first bite. The need for more vibrated through her body from where her finger pressed her lip to her belly button. She thought she would describe the food as carnal if she were writing a review. The description aligned with the name of the restaurant, Karnali.

"I am not sure any man we set you up with could compare to that," Imani joked.

"No, but half of that would still be pretty exceptional without the extra calories," Tessa added, pondering the possibilities.

"If you find half of that, I'll take it. But for now, we don't have to worry. There are several more courses of this to go." Abigail felt encouraged by the rush coursing through her body.

The women moved through each course, with the occasional comment but mostly murmurs of culinary delight.

Chapter 5

"Hmm, that was a nice appetizer," Tessa said, leading the trio out of the restaurant.

"Appetizer? That was an entire meal. There is no way you can still be hungry." Imani's disbelief seemed like an accusation.

"Hungry? Yes. For food? No. I had something a little different planned for our second course."

Abigail wondered how Tessa could sound both sinister and enticing at the same time. Whatever magical spell Tessa was conjuring moved Abigail forward. The night air felt electric on her skin. Dinner had teased a carnal appetite. Her body ached with desire and felt fuelled by the sensuality of the dining experience.

Abigail's body pulsed with effervescent vitality, and her skin tingled with excited energy. She knew she stood perched on a pinnacle. She could either turn around and retreat into the solitude of her home and safe routine or follow Tessa into the next adventure. Butterflies fluttered in her stomach with the unknown. There was no way she was not following Tessa's lead tonight.

Like the Pied Piper, Tessa led them to a club to dance the night away. The club pulsed with the beat of the music. It vibrated through the ground and travelled up her nervous system with an electrical zing. Even before they entered the building, Abigail felt the tug of the rhythm.

"Welcome to Club Ke Kino," Tessa said.

"How come I feel like there is something you are not telling us?" Despite her suspicion of Tessa, the music had a hold of her as her hips that had already begun moving a sensual pace.

"Nothing to worry about," Tessa replied, grabbing Abigail's hand and escorting her swaying body inside. Abigail grabbed Imani as they passed, forming a chain of moving forms.

As they entered, the air was heavy with the scent of exotic spices and fragrances designed to stimulate the senses. The music reverberated through their bodies, urging them to move with the rhythm and join the collection of forms on the dance floor. "Let your senses guide you!" Tessa encouraged and directed them into the center of the mob, heat emanating from the people surrounding them. A fine, cool mist fell from above, coating everything in a slippery gloss.

Abigail felt her inhibitions melt away as she moved with Tessa and Imani. The former Abigail, free-spirited and adventurous, refuses to remain imprisoned. She wanted out to play, and nothing would stop her tonight.

"Isn't this amazing?" Imani shouted over the music.

Abigail, swept up in the sensations, could only muster a mumble an "mm-hmm" as a response. Enchanted by the experience, she moved with the sensual beat of her fellow dancers like one large organism. She danced with anyone in proximity, guided by the sound of their breath, the warmth of their touch, and the enticing scents that clung to their skin.

"Abigail, take someone home tonight!" Tessa urged, her voice barely audible over the pounding music.

"Take someone home? Like a sex?" Abigail asked, her heart racing at the thought.

"Precisely! Just for fun," Tessa replied, her tone light and teased.

Abigail hesitated, her mind wrestling with the idea that old Abigail would. "I don't think I want that. This is incredible, but I want something more... meaningful. You know?"

"Yeah, I get it. But sometimes, it's fun just to let loose. Grab an ass or two." Despite not being able to see Tessa, Abigail was certain that Tessa would use the opportunity to grab someone, thankfully not Abigail herself.

"Maybe for you," Abigail replied, a small smile on her lips. "But I think I'll stick to dancing for now."

"Suit yourself," Tessa said, clearly not giving up on the idea, but turned away to focus her attention on another dancer.

Abigail continued to dance with Imani and other Club Ke Kino patrons, losing herself in the heady mix of sound, touch, and scent. It was intoxicating, enveloping her in an erotic sheath that she never wanted to leave. She felt liberated. Her dress now clung to her body, wet from the mist and her sweat trying to cool the thick heat. Hands brushed her thighs and moved to the small of her back, pulling her closer to a willing body. She rocked against the form and pressed her breasts into the man's chest, getting her head close to the crook of his neck to get a better smell, citrus, the vivacious scent. With a little flick of her tongue, she took a little taste, feeling wicked.

Abigail let out a groan of pleasure as she felt the movement of someone behind her, their body swaying and stroking her backside. Despite the potential consequences, Abigail didn't mind getting lost in this feeling. She continued moving her body to the ever-changing beat. She turned from partner to partner, uninhibited, as she explored to her heart's content.

Tessa interrupted Abigail's flow, grabbed her arm, and pulled her in close. Abigail was startled when she heard Jules whisper in her ear that Imani was also beside her. Abigail had forgotten the AI was ever present and watchful. Should she feel embarrassed? She wondered, but stopped when Tessa's laughter interrupted her thoughts.

"Ladies, sorry to leave you. Well, not really. I'm heading out with Paul. But I am sorry we didn't get to 'Operation Love Quest'. I'll contact you both tomorrow or the next day, depending on how adventurous Paul is."

Remembering her own AI companion, Abigail replied, "Be safe. Please leave your AI on at least to track where you are and figure out if Paul has a last name." Abigail was always concerned that one day, Tessa's free spirit would get her into trouble.

"Babe," Tessa said, leaning into Abigail's ear, "I never turn it off. It can listen to anything it wants. Voyeurism has its appeal." Tessa replied with a quick kiss on the cheek before shooting off.

Never turn it off, she thought. Abigail cringed. She disconnected Jules to go to the bathroom. Perhaps she shouldn't worry about what Jules sees or hears, for tonight, Abigail decided, she would leave Jules on. It is the safest thing to do.

"It looks like it's just us now," Abigail said to Imani, feeling disappointed that Tessa had so quickly found an enticing distraction. But she couldn't begrudge her friend's free-spirited nature—it was what made Tessa who she was.

Imani guided Abigail to the booths where they could sit and cool off before hitting the dance floor again. Reaching the booth, they realized it was already occupied by club goers. Each one engaged in sensual activities with the person or persons sitting next to them. Abigail hesitantly reached out, her fingers brushing against warm skin and smooth fabric, feeling the unfamiliar contours of other bodies. Abigail slid into the booth, nestling herself between two inviting figures. Similarly, Imani slid from the booth's other side.

Abigail explored with her finger and mouth, opening herself up to the sensual touches. Bodies moved and shuffled as people joined or left the group. Abigail found herself perched on someone's lap. She felt no embarrassment, only a sense of curiosity and wonder.

An unknown man traced his finger along her neck and back to her ear. Abigail purred, pushing her face into his hand to elicit more contact. Abigail could feel his warm breath as he nibbled at the same ear. Whoever he was, he was not greedy with his touches. Each touch skimmed the surface in a slow, haphazard motion. He buried his nose in her hair, taking in the scent, and repaid Abigail with a kiss at the nape of her neck.

Abigail felt the man's thumb move across her neck to the edge of her dress. He pulled the zipper down her back, loosening the top of the dress. He paused, waiting for consent before he continued. Nanosecond thoughts raced through her mind. Was she intoxicated, drugged, or impaired? The man behind her received a whispered "yes" from Abigail. She wanted this. Small kisses dotted her spine, retracing where he had opened her dress and then unfixed her bra. Abigail felt the sudden release of her breasts, which clung to the damp fabric. Abigail realized that the state of her dress mirrored her personality, technically free but clinging tight to the structure. If her dress gave way, could she?

Pushing the fabric and strap away from one shoulder, she was rewarded with more kisses and a tentative lick. As his mouth moved from the crock of her neck, he pulled down her dress from her arm. As half of her dress fell open, heat spread across her skin, knowing her breast was exposed to the elements. He moved his hands, one to her hip and the other to her abdomen, pulling back to rest on his bare chest.

A warm breath tickled at her nipple before a lick glided across the sensitive skin. It was the person to the right, exploring someone new. Abigail moaned encouragement as she slid her hand across the back of their head, pulling them in closer. The greedy mouth sucked harder. Abigail held them in position, wrapping her hand into their hair and pushing a warm face to her chest. The tug on her breast deepened, and Abigail could feel herself falling over the precipice.

Abigail grabbed at her dress, tugging it down to expose the other neglected breast. She felt relief as soon as the warm air caressed her exposed skin. The man behind her chuckled into her neck as her back arched, and she pressed harder into his lap. "Breath, I've got you," he whispered while cupping her breast. He moved his thumb across her nipple with gentle pulls, all the while nipping at her neck. As if choreographed, these two strangers guided Abigail to climax, leaving her breathless. The skilled nipple pleasurer moved on. Abigail felt a pang of guilt for not reciprocating or at least thanking the person, but her mind was exhausted and was in no position to search for them. While she recovered, the man behind Abigail held her upright and lazily caressed her body. Abigail caressed the back of his hand while it roamed. She felt safe. Safe with a nameless stranger.

The man shifted Abigail to his side, his arm draped

around her shoulder. Abigail assumed it was her turn to share and traced her hand down his chest to the waist of his pants. He stilted her hand. "No, dear, that isn't necessary."

"But I want to," and to her surprise, she did.

"I think tonight needed to be about you." He kissed her hand and returned her hand to her lap. There was a sudden void beside her as he moved away. Abigail remained stunned at the polite rejection. People moved, filling the space abruptly vacated. Her bare skin provided plenty of canvas for the next person, but their touches were unsatisfactory. Abigail moved along, finding someone else to touch and pass the time, but the connection to the collective sensuality was lost.

The bodies continued to rotate until Abigail found herself next to Imani.

"Can you imagine Tessa's reaction if she was here now?" Abigail panted. The club's sensual atmosphere flushed her cheeks. "She'd be so proud."

"Indeed, proud of you. She would likely make some comment about an Ice Princess melting to me. It would not matter. I am made of ice that burned hot tonight." Abigail considered whether it would be impolite to inquire about how hot Imani got, but chose not to pry.

"Tessa will be jealous that she missed out," Imani said, lowering her head to rest on Abigail's shoulder, too exhausted to hold it up. Aware that her dress was still down at her waist, Abigail wondered what state Imani was in.

"Abigail, can I admit something?" Imani asked. "Sometimes...I think I might fall for my AI." Imani's voice dropped to a whisper in Abigail's ear. There was no trace of humor. The statement sounded more shameful, as if it hurt to utter the admission.

"Really?" Her hand stilled on the arm of a stranger she had been caressing to focus her attention on Imani. Despite their friendship, Imani seemed aloof, in contrast to Tessa's flamboyant personality. If Imani wished to share; Abigail would pay attention.

"This is going to sound stupid. I feel like a failure every day. My job is a disappointment; there is never progress." Abigail felt a warm tear slip from Imani's face to her bare shoulder before she continued. "My features are sharp, I can feel my chin is pointy, my cheeks are hard, my breasts are small...I am the Ice Princess Tessa calls me. But my AI doesn't see me as a failure or a package of human faults. I can never disappoint it."

"Imani, your AI is programmed that way. It has learned to give you exactly what it believes you need. But it will never catch you off guard with a frantic kiss, never stoke your skin-"

"No, but I could come here for that." Abigail could feel Imani's grin against the bare shoulder. The mood lightened with a bit of humor.

"Imani, you are a sensual, brilliant woman. Ignore anyone, including Tessa, who says differently." Abigail patted Imani's hair. "Maybe we should set you up on some blind dates. There is a teacher, Mr. Simmons, who is absolutely thrilling to bump elbows with." Abigail joked, but she wondered who the perfect partner for Imani would be.

"Thank you for trusting me, Imani. I can talk to Tessa about the Ice Princess comments if you would like." Abigail offered to serve as an ambassador between the two women.

"That isn't necessary. Tessa's comments don't bother me. I know her behavior comes from her insecurities, something I doubt she is ready to accept about herself. Eventually, we'll discover a foundation for friendship."

"Imani, you are one of the most intelligent and carrying people I have ever met. I am so happy we became friends."

As they sat there, the spell they were under faded away. Abigail knew that tonight would be a night she'd never forget. And though Tessa had left them to pursue her desires, Abigail felt grateful for the friendship and support that bound the three women together, no matter where their lives led them.

With one last caress from the strangers with whom they had shared their intimacy, Abigail and Imani stood up and left the booth. Abigail struggled to pull back her damp dress. She had lost her bra on the floor, but had no intention of searching for it. They made their way to the club's exit. Outside, the cool night air contrasted with the hot atmosphere they had just left behind.

"Abigail," Imani said, looping her arm through Abigail's as they walked down the street, "Tonight was an absolute blast."

"Agree," Abigail replied, feeling the warmth of Imani's arm against hers. "It's rare that we let loose like this, if ever."

As they strolled along, their AI companions kept watch, tapping into the city's network of sensors and ensuring their safety. Abigail felt grateful for the invisible guardians that allowed them to enjoy their night without worry.

"Hey, remember our conversation about what we find attractive in people?" Abigail asked, her mind still spinning from the sensory overload she had experienced at the club.

"Of course," Imani tittered. "Exotic and spicy, or maybe the opposite. There's a pretty big range."

"Right." Her thoughts racing with possibilities. "Well, tonight helped me learn more about what I want in a partner. Someone who can make me feel alive and challenge my senses in new and exciting ways." Abigail's thoughts returned to the stranger. She felt both sexy and safe at once.

"Sounds perfect," Imani agreed, squeezing Abigail's arm. "And Tessa will be thrilled to hear it. She'll be even more determined to find you the perfect blind date now."

"I may know what I want, but one night out hasn't made me agree to this blind date shenanigans." Abigail had enjoyed letting the old her out to have fun one night, but she would lock her back up safe and sound when she got home.

"We'll see. Tessa can be very persistent. And so can I." Imani's words felt like a promise.

As they continued walking, the sounds of the city carried on around them—the distant hum of traffic, the rustling of leaves in the breeze, and the faint laughter of other revelers enjoying their night. Abigail felt alive, energized by the evening she had shared with her friends.

Abigail floated into her apartment, still in a blissful daydream from the night before. She haphazardly kicked off her heels, letting her feet be comforted by the plush carpet. However, with a violent jolt, a shudder shook her body, ripping her out of her reverie. And then she wasn't.

Her body collapsed to the floor as she gasped for air. Sobs wracked her body. The memories flooded back, causing her to convulse in pain.

Abigail's knees and palms burned, reliving how the pavement had once torn at her skin. Her body was lost in time, recalling the scattered details of her attack, the kick to her side when already down, the vile threats he hurled at her to stay still, and the stench of stale alcohol as he bent down to pull the strap of her purse. The pressure of the purse strap that had cut off her oxygen and maybe her blood supply. The final spiteful kick before he sauntered off. That night, the faceless evil stole more than her purse. He took Abigail's confidence and spirit.

What seemed like a distant voice gradually became louder and more urgent. "Abigail, breathe. You are having a panic attack. You are safe," Jules repeated.

As the spasm lessened, the soft comfort of the carpet replaced the rough edges of her memories beneath her hands. And then she could smell it - cocoa and vanilla bean, filling the room with a grounding smell. That was Jules, using a soothing scent like invisible arms.

Abigail curled up in a ball on her side, whimpering in fear. Venus took a spot at her side. The empathetic cat purred and nuzzled against her, offering her form of comfort. Tears streamed down Abigail's face as she whispered, "I was so happy." But now that happiness felt like a distant memory as she relived the traumatic event that had changed everything. "Why now? How can he still hurt me?" She spoke to the empty room, feeling alone and vulnerable. It had been years since the attack, yet it still felt raw, especially when she would relive the traumatic experience.

Jules responded calmly, "Abigail, I am not equipped to give psychological advice, but as your lifelong program companion, I can say tonight was the first time you were joyful, similar to before the attack." The AI's words brought a sense of clarity amidst the chaos of her emotions. "It may have resulted in a panic response, a form of PTSD. I can arrange another session with Dr. Patel if you would like." Abigail did not acknowledge the benevolent AI.

Abigail didn't want to consider another therapy session at that moment. While Dr. Patel had helped immensely over the years, Abigail felt the need to overcome this panic attack alone, or at least try. It was not like Dr. Patel would arrive in a few minutes to comfort her.

Abigail stayed on the living room floor, waiting for her grief to subside. The only presence in the room was her loyal cat and Jules' disembodied voice, offering reassurance. Finally, exhaustion took over, and she drifted into a slumber.

Abigail's body ached from sleeping on the hard floor, and she couldn't help but wince in pain as she woke up hours later. The only sounds in the apartment were Venus' soft snores. Carefully pushing Venus aside to avoid disturbing her, Abigail sat up and rubbed her sore muscles.

An unfamiliar emotion was rising within her, and she struggled to identify it. She knew anger. Anger towards the man who had attacked her five years ago and towards herself for hiding away. She also knew fear. The fear of it happening again. However, these two emotions were merging into another feeling. Was "pissed off" just another version of anger? It felt like anger, with a sense of determination, a purpose. Whatever it was, Abigail was tired of hiding away and living in fear. She wanted to reclaim her life, to be the sound person she used to be. She stood, heading to her room, resigned to go on a blind date, even if it was to prove to herself that she could do it.

Chapter 6

Abigail's consciousness meandered back to her as the aroma of sizzling bacon wove through the air, a sensory alarm clock more effective than any chime or buzz. The ache of her body from the night before severed to remind her of her resolve. She swung her legs over the bed's edge and pushed herself up. Once secure on her feet, she navigated towards the kitchen with practiced ease.

"Morning, Jules," she greeted the companion, whose presence was signaled by a soft, ambient hum.

"Good morning, Abigail," Jules greeted in its ever-calming tone. "Shall I start the coffee?"

"Please," she said, a smile curving at the thought of the rich, full-bodied brew that awaited her. As the coffee machine gurgled to life, she cracked eggs into a pan with a rhythm born of many such mornings, the sounds painting a vivid picture in her mind.

Memories of dinner last night echoed like a symphony in Abigail's thoughts. With each bite, unexpected textures and tastes danced across her palate.

She plated her modest breakfast, the clink of a fork on ceramic, a crisp punctuation in the quiet of her apartment. Abigail reached for her communication device, swiping deftly to send a message to Tessa. Her fingers danced across the braille display, checking in on her friend to ensure she was okay and reminding her they had her parent's anniversary party.

"Hey, Tess. Are you well?" she typed the question. She took a bite of fluffy eggs and shared a piece with her loyal cat.

Seconds later, the device vibrated, and Abigail answered Tessa's call. "More than good, absolutely blissful," Tessa chimed in her cheery digital voice. "How about you? How'd the rest of your night go?"

Slow chewing gave Abigail time to consider how much to divulge. The taste of last night's escapade lingered on her tongue, a secret sweetness, but the panic still hummed with notes of bitterness. She wasn't quite ready to share either side fully. "It was good," she replied, a master of understatement.

"Good? Just good?" Tessa's incredulity spread through the speaker. "You're holding out on me, Abi. Spill!"

"Let's just say there were... unexpected developments," Abigail teased back, her grin unseen but no less genuine. She shook the memory of the panic attack away. "But let's save it for later, okay?"

"Fine," Tessa acceded with an audible pout. "But you owe

me details. Big-time."

"Maybe," Abigail conceded, taking another sip of her coffee, its robust flavor grounding her. "Just wanted to let you know. I thought about it and will concede to a blind date." trepidation snaked through Abigail's gut, quickly replaced by enthusiasm. Saying it out loud to Tessa meant she could never backtrack. She would plunge in headfirst.

"Yeah!" Tessa shouted. She gleefully continued, "I knew we could wear you down. This will be so amazing," Tessa's joy could no longer be contained.

"Okay there, Tess. I said a blind date, not marriage." Abigail tried calming down her friend.

"Who said anything about marriage? Right now, I am aiming for a tempered kiss. that might be shocking enough for you." If Tessa found out everything that had happened last night, she would up the stakes to beyond tempered.

"Anyway, wanted to remind you about my parent's party this afternoon. I hope you can still come. I need a buffer between myself and the group's well-meaning, happily married women."

"I'll be there and can provide ample distraction."

"Distraction? I am not sure that it required more interference. Mom has asked me to ensure you are on your best behavior." Abigail chewed at her lip, waiting for Tessa's response to her behavior. Would she explode? Plot a theatrical display of just how wild she could be? Abigail resented acting as her mother's go-between; her mother could have chosen not to invite her.

"Interference then. I wouldn't want to do anything that disrupted the celebration. After all, your parents are the focus this afternoon. See you there." Tessa disconnected the communication. Abigail sat there in stunned silence, replaying Tessa's last statement over and over again in her head. The tone seemed neutral, with no hints of duplicity or sarcasm. Should she feel reassured or terrified?

Saturday mornings were meant for lounging, and today would be no different. Abigail listened to an audio show, a canned comedy meant to entertain, while she scratched Venus's back absently. Her morning had been wrapped in the warm scents of coffee and toasted bread, a sanctuary of solitude to recharge. Her phone vibrated against the countertop, reality shaking its way into her escape.

"Abigail Sorensen! Tessa just shared the news." Imani's voice crackled through the line, an excitement underlying her tone.

"Morning to you too, Imani," Abigail chuckled, her thumb caressing the edge of her cup. "Nice to see you and Tessa have something to bond over," Abigail teased. It was at least one bonus of agreeing to a date.

Imani continued missing the sarcasm and jab. "Nilesh Rao," came Imani's response, as sharp as the syringes she used in her laboratory, or at least Abigail imagined there were syringes. "He's a fellow researcher here, and I've just had the most brilliant thought."

"Does it involve equations or explosive chemicals?" Abigail jokingly retorted, unsure how she could assist Imani in her research.

"Neither. It involves you, him, and a blind date," Imani proclaimed with uncontrolled enthusiasm.

Abigail leaned back against her chair, allowing the idea to swirl around her mind and churn her gut. With anxiety coursing through her, she was still determined to proceed. She would go out with a stranger. However, she didn't need to make it easy on Imani. "But tell me, is he also a culinary connoisseur? Because after last night, my standards have skyrocketed."

"His taste might not rival that of a Michelin-starred chef, but he appreciates a good meal," Imani assured her. "But this isn't about food, Abigail. It's about connection—something I know you've been yearning for."

The words struck a chord within Abigail, resonating with a truth she couldn't deny. The longing for love's touch, its taste, was something she often cloaked behind humor. A wall of sarcasm protected her, but it felt like Imani could see the need for a connection buried in her mind's dungeon. She swirled the coffee in her mug, pondering the possibility of entwining her world with someone else's.

"Connection," Abigail echoed, allowing herself to be vulnerable about her desires. "I must admit, the idea is rather... intriguing."

"Then you'll do it?" Imani pressed, her voice tinged with

hope and something that sounded suspiciously like excitement for matchmaking.

"Tell me more about this, Nilesh," Abigail said, a playfulness creeping into her tone. "And please, spare me no detail. If I'm diving into the dating pool, I want to know if there's water in it."

"Nilesh is kind, nervous perhaps, but who wouldn't be?" Imani continued to describe Nilesh as a gentle soul with an affinity for nature.

"Sounds promising," Abigail admitted, her heart fluttering with the thrill of new beginnings. "All right, Imani. Set it up. What is the worst that can happen? He isn't your boss or anything that could make this awkward."

"No, just a colleague in a different department. There is no conflict. I knew I could count on you to take a leap of faith," Imani said, her relief palpable. "I'll message Nilesh to confirm and call you back to discuss the details." Imani sounded joyful. Maybe she should go on this date.

"Okay, Imani, talk to you soon," Abigail ended the call. She restrained herself from launching into a happy dance, but the fact was, she was delighted. It was a first step; maybe it would lead to disaster, but at least she was moving forward.

A few minutes later, her communication device chirped. As expected, it was Imani, but without plans for the night.

"Abigail," Imani's voice reverberated through the phone, trepidation in her voice. "Before I forget, I should mention something about Nilesh."

"Ah, the plot thickens. Is he an alien sent to Earth to

observe our customs?" Abigail suggested.

"Um, no, that's not it—" Imani started, but Abigail came up with another outlandish idea.

"Is he a time traveler from the future, here to right a terrible wrong that destroys the planet, but of course, he needs a brief romance on the side?" Abigail enjoyed this far too much, so early in the morning.

"He's... well, he's the nervous type. It might take him a bit to warm up at the start," Imani admitted, a note of caution threading her otherwise confident tone.

"Like an oven," Abigail said, adjusting her position on the couch to lounge out. It was Saturday, after all. "Requires a bit of patience before it's at the perfect temperature."

"Exactly!" Imani exclaimed, relieved. "You have such a way with words, Abigail. But yes, give him time. Once he's comfortable, he's quite the conversationalist."

"Time is something I can offer."

"Fantastic! I knew you'd understand. He is a great guy, just a little shy at first." There was a rustle on the other end of the line, likely Imani's lab coat brushing against the receiver. "He is good meeting tomorrow. How does that sound?" Imani inquired flatly, as if she was finding time for Abigail to meet with the dentist.

"Tomorrow, that is so soon. I guess I am free in the late afternoon." Abigail answered, but her voice rose at the end like a question.

"So that is a yes," Imani confirmed, not wanting to give Abigail the chance to back out.

"It's a yes," Abigail confirmed.

Imani got immediately to business, "any thoughts on where you'd like to meet him?"

Abigail pondered, the coffee's bitter tang still on her tongue. "A new coffee shop opened up downtown, The Jumping Bean. Rumor has it the pastries are to die for."

"Sounds perfect. A relaxed atmosphere might help Nilesh ease into things," Imani mused, the sound of papers shuffling betraying her multitasking nature.

"Exactly my thought. He can take in the scent of vanilla bean and cinnamon swirls rather than whatever anxiety smells like." Abigail chuckled, imagining the quaint little shop as the backdrop for their encounter.

"Anxiety has a smell? Enlighten me."

Abigail coughed on her coffee, surprised that Imani was getting in on the verbal banter. Enthusiasm was contagious this morning.

"Like the smell of burned toast and ammonia, if my nose doesn't deceive me."

"Let's save you from that fate, then. The Jumping Bean, tomorrow, say 3 p.m.?" Imani proposed, her voice taking on a note of excitement.

"Tomorrow at 3 p.m. sounds good," Abigail nodded, feeling the possibilities weaving around her heart.

"Great, I'll suggest Nilesh get there a little early to give himself time to settle in. Let the jittery electrons in his system dissipate a bit."

"Perfect. And Imani... thanks for playing matchmaker."

"Of course, Abigail. Who knows? This could be the start of something... electric." Imani's attempt at humor crackled through the line.

"Electric or not, I'm looking forward to meeting him," Abigail said genuinely.

"I'll send Nilesh a message to confirm tomorrow. Is there anything else you need?" Imani was back in dental reception mode.

"Nope, that's all. Talk to you later, Imani". Abigail said as she disconnected the call.

"Electric," she whispered to herself, the corners of her mouth tilting upwards. If nothing else, tomorrow promised to be an exciting day.

Chapter 7

The spring air was excruciatingly warm, and for the hundredth time, Abigail cursed her choice of outfit. While the dress fabric felt light, it provided little ventilation and did not absorb the icky sweat trickling down her skin. It took pure willpower not to rip her clothing off. Naked would be better than the icky feeling of repeated layers of sweat.

"Well, this is quite the party," Tessa said, coming up from behind Abigail.

"Oh, thank goodness you are here. Any chance you have a change of clothing with you? This dress is driving me bonkers. There is nothing in my old bedroom except for a Cinderella-type prom dress, which might be the only thing worse than this dress."

"No, but I will happily raid your mother's closet with you." Tessa offered to be an accomplice to the minor crime.

"The house is off limits." A stern voice interrupted before Abigail could agree. Her mother came close. "I want the two of you on your best behavior. I have lookouts specifically for you both this afternoon." Unfortunately, Gwen Sorensen's icy demeanor did nothing to cool Abigail's overheated skin. If anything, it made her skin ache as her cells noticed her mother's looming presence.

"You have AI's babysitting us? It's not like we are going to take off with the silverware. I just wanted a change of clothes." Abigail felt reduced to a knotty teenager. It was amazing how quickly her mother could get the upper hand.

"If you didn't behave like children, I wouldn't need to treat you like children. You can manage with your current outfit; change is unnecessary. Perhaps this will serve as a lesson to plan better. I came over to let you know a special guest has arrived. I expect you to be pleasant."

A wave of concern overtook Abigail. Dread clung to the back of her throat, cutting off her ability to breathe for a long second. No good would result from a special guest.

Before Abigail could ask who the person was, Jules interrupted. "Abigail, Ryker has entered the yard." Goosebumps pricked her already sensitive skin, and her stomach sunk.

"What the hell!" Abigail exclaimed in disbelief. "You invited Ryker?"

"Watch your volume, young lady. You are practically hysterical," her mother chided. "Yes, Ryker used to be a dear friend of the family. A celebration of marriage is the perfect place for the two of you to start anew."

Abigail felt like her skin was buzzing with pent-up fury, overshadowing the previous sticky feeling. How dare her mother blindside her like this? She sensed Tessa's hand on her arm, offering silent support. Even Tessa was afraid to go toe-to-toe with Gwen Sorensen.

Venom dripped from Abigail's next words: "How dare you!" Her quiet but angered tone shocked even herself. It felt like a beast was clawing its way up from her chest, out of her mouth, blinded by fury.

"Stop being so dramatic and get a hold of yourself. You will thank me one day." Abigail's mother dismissed her daughter's rage.

Abigail could feel the low guttural growl vibrate through her body and out, pushing its way out of her mouth and nose in a menacing wheeze. "I will not get a hold of myself. You crossed a line that you had no business even being near. I might not be in a relationship right now, but at least I am not still with a spineless fragile coward who disappeared when I needed him the most. What made you think I would want to go back down that road? Don't answer that. I don't want to know what you were thinking." Abigail shook with anger and hurt.

"Abi, honey. I am only looking out for your future. Ryker says he has grown and wants to try again." Her mother's smooth tone tried to diffuse the situation as if Abigail was still a wild child who could be tamed by her mother's voice.

"If he had changed, he wouldn't be a spineless coward who needed my mother to arrange a meeting." Abigail spat in response.

"Solid burn," Tessa said. She never endorsed Ryker. Abigail appreciated Tessa's support. There was little chance that her mother would redirect her attention to Tessa at this moment, but Tessa had still braved the possibility to offer her support.

"Mom, think about it. Remember when my windpipe was so bruised I couldn't speak? When it hurt to cry? You remember that. Who was the asshole that left me? Who complained that my pain was too much for him to manage?" Abigail's voice wavered, losing the steam that had fueled her.

"Of course I remember, Abigail. It was a terrible time for all of us. But Ryker is willing to take you back now. You should feel grateful he still cares."

There was no way her mother was listening to her—or maybe she wasn't listening to herself—because each word she spoke reignited Abigail's anger. "Grateful? I don't want him back." Abigail enunciated each syllable of the words, trying to drive the meaning into her mother.

Frustrated by her mother's inability to understand the magnitude of her mistake, Abigail decided it was time to play the trump card. "Does Dad know what you have done?" she said in a frigid tone.

"Well, no. I don't see what business it is of his."

"Perhaps because he would also be livid with your meddling. Do you think Dad would want Ryker back in our lives? Is Ryker the son-in-law he always wanted?"

"Abigail. I get you are upset. But Ryker is here now. Why

not go see what can be rekindled?" Abigail noted the desperation in her mother's voice to recover somehow.

"Let me make this clear. I do not, under any circumstances, want to speak to Ryker now or ever. Tessa and I are going to go inside and stand in front of an open freezer to cool off. Have a splendid party, Mother." She turned, adjusting Tessa's unwavering grip on her arm, and marched off. She was thankful when Jules advised her she was going in the right direction to the house. If she had to turn back and go in the opposite direction, her power would have diminished slightly.

"OMG. That was amazing. I don't think I have ever heard you speak to anyone like that, and that was your mother. You are my hero." Tessa's words beamed with pride.

"I think I am going to be sick. Let's get inside," Abigail wheezed. The adrenaline was subsiding, and the reality of the confrontation with her mother was coming into focus.

True to her word, Abigail went directly to the freezer, opened the door, and used it as a large fan to push the cold air into her damp skin. She rifled through the contents to find a small cold package to press to her skin.

"I can't believe I said all of that," Abigail spoke to the inside of the freezer.

"You did, and it was exceptional. It was so amazing that I wish I had an audio recording to play it back."

"I believe I'm going to vomit," Abigail said again into the freezer.

"Deep breaths, it will pass. But if you want to puke in your mom's freezer, go ahead." Tessa rubbed her back in a large circular motion to help Abigail calm her nerves.

Abigail laughed at Tessa's suggestion, helping to ease the tension in her body. "I have never spoken to my mother like that. Even as a teenager." Exhaustion set in, and she slid to the floor, shifting to lean back on the fridge. Tessa scooted down beside her, and they fell silent for a few minutes.

"I can't believe she did that. Ambush me with Ryker."

"That was extreme, even for your mom. I am sorry that happened."

"Oh, I should have told her I have a date planned for tomorrow. With a scientist. That would have thrown her off a bit." Abigail tried to sound tough, but her statement fell a little flat compared to the dialogue that had just transpired between them.

"You have a date tomorrow? Why am I just hearing about it now?" Tessa latched on to the latest information.

"I thought Imani would have told you. I assumed you both were in constant conversation about my dating prospects."

"No, but I didn't answer one of Imani's calls. Perhaps she would have shared," Tessa admitted.

"Serves you right for ignoring Imani. I wish the two of you could get along."

"We are warming up to each other. It helps that we have interloped into your personal life as a bonding experience."

"I am thrilled my lack of love life has given you both common ground. Please put it to good use."

As they sat on the kitchen floor, the sound of the backyard door opening and closing interrupted them. For a moment, Abigail froze in fear that Ryker had just entered. To her relief, her father's comforting voice called out for her. "Over here, on the floor by the fridge," she replied to her dad.

"Are you hurt?" Concern in his voice as he moved closer to where Abigail and Tessa sat.

"No, just cooling off," she reassured him. While Abigail loved both of her parents and knew they loved her too, she had always been more relaxed around her dad. She felt an icy bit guilty for pulling the dad card with her mom a few minutes ago. One thing that made Gwen Sorensen insecure was feeling like an inferior parent.

"Oh, good. I wanted to let you know Ryker was at the party so you would not be surprised. Your mother must have invited everyone on her contact list."

Abigail felt relief that her father's good nature didn't assume the worst of her mother. Despite what had happened, she did not want to cause conflict for her parents on such an important day. The Ryker issue would remain between her mom and herself. "Thanks for letting me know," Abigail said to her dad. "I'll be out in a bit."

"Ok, honey," her dad replied before he returned to the party. Why couldn't it be this easy with her mother?

Tessa interrupted her thoughts: "Want to raid your parent's liquor cabinet? I am sure they still have the Crème de Menthe bottle. No one ever drinks that stuff." Tessa elbowed Abigail. "We could try on the prom dress and feel like teenagers again?"

Abigail laughed at the idea. "I didn't enjoy being a teenager the first time. As much as I want to hide away in my bedroom, I should probably head back so the aunties can all tell me how much happier I would be if I got married."

"Let's tell them we are engaged," Tessa suggested. "That should get them off your back."

"A sweet offer, but no one would believe Tessa Sato decided to settle down. I have ample experience navigating the aunties."

"Don't forget there is a Ryker to contend with. Maybe hiding isn't a horrible thing."

Even his name, Ryker, pained Abigail. She was certain she didn't want him back. But she couldn't figure out what caused more pain, the fact he left her when she was hurt or all the time they were together, happy yet unaware he was the wrong person for her. "If anyone asks, I am dating a scientist named Nilesh. That should spread through the party pretty quickly." It's not a lie, but a misinterpretation of the truth.

"Actually, scratch that. I will tell the first person I speak to, and then we can leave this party. I will make us something better to eat than this catered blah food." Abigail would claw back her power from her mother, Ryker, and anyone else who made her feel small.

Chapter 8

That evening, Abigail lay in bed tossing and turning, her thoughts chaotic with anticipation and trepidation. Her muttering punctuated the silent hum of the night only. "What will we even talk about?" hugging a pillow close to her chest. A warm breeze from the open window played across her face, carrying with it the fragrance of night-blooming jasmine—a bittersweet reminder of romantic possibilities that seemed tantalizingly close and achingly out of reach.

"Jules," she appealed into the darkness.

"Yes, Abigail?" The AI's voice materialized, soothing and steady.

"Am I overthinking this? What if there's no spark... or what if there's an inferno?"

"Both are equally fascinating outcomes," Jules replied with programmed empathy. "Chemistry is not quantifiable, but it is discoverable."

"What? Chemistry is both quantifiable and discoverable. Science is predictable. Well, most of the time." Abigail sat up in bed, intending to scold Jules on the scientific principles.

"Relationship chemistry is not quantifiable. Though many have tried, there is no science to relationship chemistry. Apologies for the confusion." Jules reassured Abigail.

"Ah, that chemistry. I just don't want to fizzle out or explode on impact." Abigail rolled over on her back, letting out a frustrated growl. "What the hell is wrong with me? I am acting like an excitable teenager. This should not be so stressful."

"Shall I review calming techniques with you?" Jules offered.

"Maybe in the morning," she said, turning onto her side and tossing the pillow across the room. She tucked her knees closer to her chest and took long, even breaths in and out. Sleep eventually claimed her. Her dreams were conversations that flowed like honey, sweet and sticky. Would she navigate the sweet liquid or drown in a thick sap?

The light of day had no visual hold on Abigail, but she felt its presence in the warm energy around her as she began preparing for the day. Her hands moved deftly, brushing her teeth, then comically missing her mouth with the toothpaste on the second attempt. "Whoops!" she exclaimed, her nose scrunching at the minty freshness adorning her cheek instead.

"Slower movements may yield better results," Jules chided.

"Where's the fun in that?" Abigail teased back, wiping her face clean before proceeding with more caution.

Abigail decided on eggs and bacon for breakfast. The sizzle of frying food filled her tiny kitchen, followed by a startled yelp as hot oil popped unexpectedly. "Ouch! Betrayed by breakfast," she scolded the frying pan with a scowl. Breakfast did not usually attack.

"Please exercise care, Abigail. Injury is not an ideal accessory for a first date," Jules reminded her, the concern in the AI's tone almost human.

"Point taken, Jules," she conceded. Her smile returned as she plated her food.

She was dressed in a soft blouse and comfortable trousers. The fabric skimmed her skin as she moved. Selecting clothes she couldn't see always felt like a game—one where texture and comfort were the rules she played by.

"You look lovely, Abigail," Jules flattered her.

"That compliment goes to my style, guru. Oh, wait, that would be you," Abigail retorted, pleased the AI appreciated her look even though no one would ever see it.

Abigail reached for her coffee cup and accidentally dipped her sleeve into the brew. "And now I'm wearing it, too. Perfect."

"Perhaps consider a shorter sleeve next time," Jules joked, the humor in their voice as dry as Abigail's other sleeve.

"Always the practical one," she laughed, dabbing at the spill.

"Practicality has its charms."

"Indeed, it does, Jules. Indeed, it does." She took a slow sip of her coffee, letting the warmth seep into her bones and steady her nerves. And with that, she was ready—three hours ahead of her date, but at least she was ready.

Abigail paced the length of her living room. Although she planned to wear sandals, her feet were still bare, and she sank into the plush carpet with each step. As she walked, she ticked off potential conversation topics on her fingers.

"So, Nilesh likes science. I could ask him about his favorite element on the periodic table." Pivoting to turn direction, Abigail changed her mind. "But then he might ask mine, and there is no way I could choose just one, and I might come across as indecisive or, worse, unintelligent."

"Abigail, you are intelligent. It is also okay to have multiple favorite elements. Could you ever pick just one ice cream flavor?" Jules's level-headed voice replied.

"Nope, having two or more flavors in a serving is superior. Maybe we should avoid ice cream flavors as well." She attempted another turn and bumped her shin into an end table.

"I searched for common questions to get to know someone. You should avoid politics, religion, and money. Music, pets, and hometowns would be acceptable initial questions."

"Ah, perfect! I'll ask about his favorite composer... and if he's more of a cat or dog person. Oh, and Imani said he likes nature."

"Careful around the coffee table," Jules warned, just in time for Abigail to sidestep the obstacle.

"Thanks, Jules. Where would I be without you?" Not waiting for an answer, she continued her mental rehearsal. Absorbed in her musings, Abigail brushed past the sideboard, where a vase of fresh gerberas perched precariously on the edge. Her elbow caught it, and in a clatter of chaos, water cascaded over the vase and splashed across the front of her trousers.

"Bloody-" She couldn't help but laugh at the absurdity, the tension releasing from her shoulders like steam from a kettle.

"It appears your outfit has taken a swim," Jules exaggerated.

"Quite the dive, indeed." Abigail wiped her hands down her now-damp clothing. "Well, no use crying over spilled water, right? Besides, it's not like anyone will see it, anyway."

"True, visibility is not a concern," Jules concurred. "However, comfort might be. Shall I assist you in selecting another ensemble?"

"Let's not fuss over it. A quick pat down, and good as new!" Abigail waved off the offer, the smile lingering on her lips.

"Very well. Your optimism remains unsoaked."

"Got to keep my spirits buoyant—it's a blind date, after all." Abigail's grin widened, her heart lighter than it had been all morning. Every touch, taste, sound, and smell took on greater significance without sight. In this unforeseen moment, the chilly dampness of her clothes reminded her that life's little surprises weren't obstacles. They were anecdotes in the making.

"Should I prepare a towel, just in case?" Jules inquired, ever the pragmatic companion.

"Only if it doubles as a cape. Every heroine needs one when venturing into the great unknown of romance," Abigail teased, heading towards the door with renewed vigor, ready to face whatever the date—and fate—had in store.

Chapter 9

Abigail arrived at The Jumping Bean Café, and with Jules's help, she navigated to the café door. A bell jingled overhead as it opened. The Jumping Bean café was a hive of the future, buzzing with the clinks and whirs of automated baristas crafting lattes meant to delight the gods, not just mere humans. A sound system crisscrossed the ceiling, bathing patrons in a soft whirl of old-world Parisian music. The rich aroma of roasted Arabica mingled with the subtle hint of ozone from the ever-present technology. Three walls of the café were in glass, which allowed the afternoon sun to warm the café to a cozy temperature. The additional warmth in the café acted like a blanket holding in the rich aroma of the café's beverages and baked goods.

"Abigail, the third table on your left has an occupant matching Nilesh's description," Jules chimed in Abigail's earpiece, its voice a soothing blend of synthetic warmth and calculated cadence.

"Thanks, Jules. You're sure it's him?" Abigail asked, her hand brushing against the smooth contours of the tables as she navigated through the cozy chaos.

"Biometric sensors don't lie, Abigail. Well, usually. I cross-referenced his public social profile image. Statistically speaking, it's a match," Jules said with an efficient digital tone.

"Statistically, huh? That's reassuring," Abigail muttered to Jules now that they were within earshot of the occupied table.

"Nilesh Rao?" she asked, reaching the table, extending her hand in the general direction of where she sensed another presence.

"Ye—Yes! Yes, Abigail Sorensen, right?" Nilesh stumbled over his words like a dancer with two left feet, finally grasping her hand, which trembled slightly. "It's a pleasure to meet you. I mean, it is you, isn't it? Not some random person I'm accosting?"

"Yes, a pleasure." Abigail's fingers caught the nervous energy in his handshake. "And you're not accosting. I'd say it's more of a cordial greeting."

"Right, cordial. I can do cordial," Nilesh muttered before clearing his throat. "Would you like to sit? The chai here is cybernetically enhanced, or so they claim—it tastes like...hmm, the only way I can describe it is as the comfort of bedtime stories as a child."

"Sounds poetic and lovely. I want to feel that way again.

I will take a cup," Abigail said, easing into her chair with a grace that belied her lack of sight.

"Jules, please go silent for a bit," she whispered, not wanting the AI to intrude on her attempt at human connection.

"Understood. Enjoy your date, Abigail. I'll be here if you need me," Jules assured her before going quiet, the electronic buzz in her ear dissipating like a ghost.

Nilesh fumbled with the menu tablet, muttering with each mistake and correction. Abigail listened intently, building a picture of him from the hesitant rhythm of his speech and the occasional brush of fabric as he shifted in his seat.

"Sorry, I'm not usually this. . well, maybe I am, but only on days ending with 'y'," Nilesh confessed, laughing off his nerves.

"Relax, Nilesh. There's no right way to do this." She felt her own nerves dissipate when immersed in Nilesh's waves of unease. It was as if his emotions were fraying like an old towel. Imani had said he was nervous, but Abigail had not expected someone to jump at his own voice.

"So, tell me about your love for nature. Imani mentioned it." She figured this would be an easy topic to start a conversation.

"Ah, yes, the great outdoors. I love to head out to a nature reserve or hiking trail," he stuttered the first few words, but a genuine fondness replaced his anxiety by the end. "The sound of leaves and the smell of earth have a certain charm. It's grounding, you know?" Abigail felt empowered by selecting a topic that dramatically impacted Nilesh's comfort level. Perhaps she was far better at blind dates than she had thought.

"Sounds wonderful. I don't get out of the town much. City girl."

"Maybe I can show you sometime. I mean, if you'd like," Nilesh ventured, a hopeful note threading his voice.

"Perhaps," Abigail said. As charming as his offer was, she was not committing her clumsy self to an outdoor adventure invitation.

As they waited for their drinks, Abigail absorbed the café's ambiance. It invoked a sense of being in Paris, a city of love. It might work out on this date. Could romance be written in the stars or brewed in a cup of cyber-chai?

Abigail's fingertips danced over the table's textured surface, tracing the grooves and whorls in the wood as a genuine laugh bubbled from her throat. "You named your houseplant?"

"Absolutely," Nilesh replied with an earnestness that had his voice teetering on the edge of excitement. "Herbert is more than a plant. He's a stoic companion in my urban jungle."

"Herbert," Abigail repeated, amusement lacing her words. "Well, I can't say I've been formally introduced to a fern before."

"First time for everything," he quipped, and they both

laughed—a sound mingling with the hum of conversation and clinking of cups around them.

"True," Abigail conceded, the warmth in her belly not entirely because of the steaming mug she cradled between her palms. There was an easiness weaving into the fabric of their interaction, a soothing rhythm punctuated by smiles she could hear in Nilesh's tone.

But then, it was there again—that scent. It brushed against her senses like a discordant note in a melody, out of place amidst the coffee aromas and the faint tang of lemon from the pastry display. She inhaled deeply, trying to separate the fragrance layers to identify the unwelcome guest.

"Is something wrong?" Nilesh's voice sliced through her concentration, tinged with concern.

"Oh, no, it's just..." Abigail hesitated, her nose wrinkling as the scent grew more robust, its origin elusive. "There's an odd smell. Do you notice it?" She hoped it was anything but him—the thought of connecting such a peculiar odor to the kind man across from her was disappointing.

"Smell?" He sounded genuinely puzzled, which only deepened her confusion. "I don't—well, I'm not sure. Maybe it's coming from outside?"

"Maybe," she agreed, though the assertion did little to convince her. The aroma was invasive, a chemical floral blend that seemed to cling stubbornly to the air between them. She tried redirecting her focus to Nilesh's words, his stories about weekend hikes, and identifying bird sounds.

"That sounds incredible," she said, a part of her mind

still wrestling with the olfactory mystery. "The world has so many beautiful secrets to share, right?"

"It does." Nilesh's voice carried a smile tinged with the awkwardness Nilesh would never entirely dispel. "And I hope to share some of those secrets with you."

Abigail smiled. I think he is trying to flirt with me, she thought. Nilesh was not smooth or charismatic, but he seemed genuine. She could probably process her thoughts better without the juxtaposition of odors assaulting her senses. She smelled her chai beverage, hoping the potent scent could reset her senses and the odor would disappear. Regrettably, the smell still hung in the air, maybe even on her clothing. Frustrated, Abigail sipped her drink, letting the taste comfort her. At the same time, she continued the conversation, all the while wondering if this invisible cloud was an omen of mismatched chemistry or simply a curious case of misplaced cologne.

"Is it just me, or does the air seem... flavored?" Abigail ventured, her voice laced with growing unease.

"Flavored?" Nilesh echoed, his tone buoyant and at ease. "I guess you could say that. The café's ambiance is quite... aromatic."

"It's more than just the café. It smells like musty old books in a library that still holds the stale scent of the years of offenses, cigars, and pipes that were once acceptably burned in the confined space." Abigail practically spat the words out in disgust. "Nilesh, do you mind if we open the café window?" Abigail asked, already moving her hand to the glass at her side.

"Of course. A little fresh air may clear away the stuffiness." Abigail had already pushed open the nearest window before Nilesh had finished his response. A breeze slipped in, offering a brief respite before being overpowered once more by his relentless fragrance campaign.

"Better?" he asked after a few moments.

"Somewhat," Abigail conceded, though the battle of bouquets waged on.

"So, I take it the smell of knowledge institutes is not your scent of choice. What smells do you find pleasing?"

Abigail considered the question. In recent days, she wondered a lot about it. Plenty of smells were pleasant. Some evoked memories or emotions, but was there any one scent that stood out above all else? "I enjoy warm scents while cooking, for example, cinnamon, rosemary, and even curries," Abigail started. Strangely, the smell of apple pie spread across the café. Abigail wondered if they had just pulled some apple and cinnamon pastries out of the oven. Perhaps it was mind over matter. The offense library was clearing away, and Abigail could now pick up on the bakery portion of the café.

Clearing her throat to continue the conversation, the smell of curry mentally knocked Abigail over. "What the...curry? You must tell me you can smell curry!" Abigail exclaimed, feeling like she was losing touch with reality.

"Oh, yes, for sure. I smell curry," Nilesh agreed. "It is probably the restaurant across the street. They have probably started preparing the stews for tonight's dinner. Intoxicating, isn't it?" Nilesh asked, pleased he could provide the answer to this odor. "Indian food is so sensual. Eating with your hands, all the different spices," Nilesh continued, unphased by the sudden arrival of the curry smells.

Stunned, Abigail took a moment to collect herself. She sipped her drink again, its robust flavor now tainted with the flavor of apples and curry. What is going on?

Unaware of Abigail's growing discomfort, Nilesh continued. "I am a bit of an aromachologist, dabbling in the science of smell and its role in human responses." His enthusiastic tone made Nilesh's excitement on the topic clear.

"I didn't realize that was a hobby. Have you always been interested in fragrances?" Abigail asked before choking on a sudden influx of pungent citrus overlaid with floral notes.

"Uh, recently," Nilesh admitted, a flush creeping into his voice. "Scent can be powerful, don't you think? Evocative."

"Powerful and evocative," she repeated, unsure what to say. Her chest tightened as the layers of aroma coalesced into a cloying fog around them. Panicking, Abigail launched her head out the window, gasping for air. Thank goodness the window was wide enough, or she would indeed have crashed through the glass with the force of her lunge.

Through coughing fits and sneezing, Abigail quietly heard, "Maybe it's too much," in Nilesh's sweet and humble tone.

Recovering, Abigail sat back in her chair, fingers tracing the outline of her mug, the ceramic cool against her skin. The pervasive scent—no, scents—still lingered around her like invasive vines, ready to choke out the life in a once-peaceful garden. Abigail was determined to uncover the nefarious plot.

"Nilesh," she began, a sweetness in her voice setting him at ease. "I'm curious about the variety of aromas here. Is it a special event at the café today?"

"Event?" He sounded genuinely perplexed, a note of concern threading his voice. "No, no special event. Just us. Why do you ask?"

Abigail chose her words carefully, not wanting to accuse Nilesh directly, but convinced the "aromachologist" knew more than he was letting on. "Oh, nothing, just such a kaleidoscope of smells this afternoon. It was like nothing I had ever experienced before." Her voice did not betray the disgust she was experiencing. "It's all overwhelming," she said tactfully. She let her words hang in the air, waiting for his response.

"Overwhelming," Nilesh repeated, defeat clinging to the word. She could hear him shuffling and then the soft ding of metal or glass being placed on the table between them. "Ah," Nilesh murmured, his cheeks flushing with a heat that Abigail could nearly feel across the small space dividing them. "I might have... well, I wanted to make sure it smelled nice." He chuckled, the sound edged with embarrassment. "So, I mixed a few things."

"Mixed?" A one-word response meant to encourage Nilesh to continue with a more detailed explanation.

"Well, I wanted the date to go well. I thought enhancing the date with pleasant smells would help us both feel more at ease." he started the explanation.

"Nilesh, what did you do?" Frustrated at what she heard, Abigail needed Nilesh to come clean immediately.

Words rushed from him in response to the command, and Nilesh continued: "I used an atomizer and small bottles of scents and spritzed our date." He sighed as if the admission suddenly released the tension in his body.

"Spritzed our date," Abigail responded, trying to keep her voice calm but suppressing the need to laugh and yell simultaneously.

Now absolved of his deceit, Nilesh touched the unseen vials and continued, "This one is 'Ocean's Embrace,' and this is 'Homemade Apple Pie.' Then there is 'Citrus Oasis,' 'Spiced Journey,'..." Nilesh's voice trailed off as he laid out the culprits on the table, a veritable buffet of bottled intentions.

"Wow," she said, a mixture of hurt, amusement, and maybe even sympathy whirling in her mind. "That's quite the expedition you've prepared for us."

"Sorry," he sighed, gathering the bottles back into his pocket with a rueful shake. "I guess I got carried away. I just wanted to impress you." Nilesh's voice sounded like he was speaking to the table. It only took a moment for the date to shift from quirky conversation to uncomfortable silence.

Abigail felt confused. He had been purposeful in deceiving her. Not that he used the atomizer and blindsided her with the aromatic assault; that wasn't the issue. The problem was that he lied when she asked about the smells. People use scents all the time to set a mood, but lying to her was wrong. But now, Nilesh seemed like a remorseful puppy dog, and Abigail was hesitant to cause him further discomfort.

"Nilesh," Abigail reached out, finding his hand and squeezing it, "you don't need all this." She waved both of her unseen hands, wishing she could use a finger to jab his pockets, now stuffed with scented ambitions. "Just being here would have been more than enough."

"Really?" he asked, hope flickering in his voice.

"Really," she affirmed, her touch lingering on his hand for a moment longer, an unspoken reassurance. "Let's just enjoy our coffee, okay? And maybe get a slice of real apple pie."

"Right, yes," Nilesh agreed quickly, the relief in his voice palpable as he opened another window, inviting a gust of unscented clarity into the Jumping Bean café.

As Abigail savored the last few bites of her apple pie, she felt remorse for what she knew would come next. A gust of fresh air flowed into the Jumping Bean café, and Abigail tilted her head towards the source of the breeze, appreciating the reprieve. She could hear the faint hustle of the urban jungle outside—the whir of electric cars gliding past and the intermittent laughter from passersby accepting the distraction a few minutes longer.

"Abigail," Nilesh began, bringing Abigail back to the present moment. "I—I'm not very good at this sort of thing," his tone now stripped of its earlier enthusiasm,

"Hey, it's all right." Abigail's voice was soft but steady. "You know, something is endearing about your... let's call it 'scent-sational' approach."

Nilesh chuckled, a sound that trembled on the edge of genuine joy and lingering embarrassment. "Endearing? You're probably the first to describe my nervous blunders that way."

"Then I'll take that as a compliment to my originality," she said with a playful tilt of her head, her lips curving into a smile that she hoped he could feel rather than see.

"Abigail, you're too kind," he murmured, his hand turning to clasp hers, a silent plea for forgiveness conveyed through the warmth of his palm.

"Kindness has nothing to do with it," she replied, her thumb tracing circles on the back of his hand. "It's just honesty."

The conversation lulled. Nilesh fidgeted in his seat, the faux leather creaking under his shifting weight. For a moment, Abigail considered ordering more food to postpone the inevitable, which would give him false hope. She knew how this date would end.

"Nilesh," Abigail ventured, her voice soft but steady. "I've enjoyed our conversation this afternoon."

"Really?" His word was an eager puppy, tail wagging in the dark.

"Yes, but I think—"

"Would you like to do this again?" Nilesh interjected, his nerves jangling like loose change in his voice.

Abigail exhaled, a breath she didn't realize she'd been holding. The scent that clung to him still clawed at her senses, and his little deception echoed louder than his words.

"Nilesh, you're a wonderful person, and I'm flattered, but I don't think we're quite the right fit for each other," she said, her tone laced with regret yet firm.

"Is it... is it because of the scents? I am sorry!" There was a desperation in his voice.

Abigail shook her head, a tiny smile gracing her lips despite the situation. "I know you feel sorry and didn't mean to cause me harm. But honestly, it was manipulative, and it is not how I would want to start a relationship."

He sat back in his chair, deflated. "I understand. Thank you for being so kind about it."

"Thank you for understanding," she replied. "And Nilesh, the next person you date, be honest. If they are the right fit for you, they would also want to play with the scents." They parted with a handshake that was more solemn than cordial, a silent agreement that this chapter had closed as swiftly as it had opened.

Back in the solitude of her apartment, Abigail dialed Imani's number, her fingers dancing over the braille-labeled buttons of her phone.

"Hey, Imani, it's Abigail.' Her voice carried a mixture of disappointment and amusement.

"Hey! How did it go with Nilesh, our lovable nervous Nellie?" Imani's voice chuckled at the description of Nilesh.

"Let's just say he was generous with his fragrances," Abigail teased, not wanting to go into the details. Abigail curled her feet beneath her on the sofa.

"Generous? I feel like there is much more to the story than just a smell," Imani's curiosity peaked. "Was it that bad?"

"It was more than one odor. It was like being inside a perfume bottle factory during an earthquake. But honestly, I'm glad I went," Abigail confessed, tracing the textured fabric of her couch.

"First one down, right? It'll get easier," Imani encouraged, comfortingly patting her voice on the back.

"Exactly," Abigail affirmed, her spirits lifting. "There's always the next—"

Her words were cut short by a notification chime from her phone. A message from Tessa buzzed, activating the screen in bold electronic braille:

"Tuesday night, 8 PM, the bar at 2nd and Church, Mark Rivera," Abigail read aloud.

"Got another date lined up already?" Imani's inquisitiveness was audible through the phone line.

"It seems like it," Abigail said, a grin on her lips. Tessa's relentless.

"Good luck. Maybe consider bringing a nose plug." Imani joked.

"Will do," Abigail laughed, ending the call with a newfound optimism.

Chapter 10

Tuesday morning, Abigail met Tessa at their usual pre-work café. Staying clear of coffee, however, she ordered a steaming cup of chamomile tea. Abigail continued, "Riley said what?" her voice tinged with disbelief and amusement as Tessa's morning story.

"Can you believe it? My own AI dares to criticize my neck, double-chin indeed." Abigail could hear Tessa's hands theatrically flying about. Her hands struck the table, and Abigail swore she could feel a breeze as they shot back up in the air. Tessa was agitated. That morning, Riley, the rogue home assistant AI, had overstepped its bounds.

"Maybe it's projecting its insecurities," Abigail kidded, the corners of her mouth twitching upwards. She could almost sense Tessa rolling her eyes, a gesture she had learned to detect in the cadence of her friend's voice.

"Right? Since when did AIs become fashion critics?" Tessa

huffed. "And for your information, I switched outfits three times just to spite it."

"Three times, huh? That's quite the act of rebellion." Abigail's tone was dry, with a flavor of mock seriousness.

"Oh, that is not all. I gave Riley a lecture on the consequences of body shaming and let it know that there has never been a complaint in bed about my chin. After all, a man is usually grabbing my ass or my boobs." Both women erupted in laughter at the rant.

"Hopefully, Riley has learned its lesson. It provided excessive compliments for the rest of the morning. Likely compensating for its faux pas," Tessa said, accepting the caffeine-infused drink that had arrived at their table.

"Anyway," Tessa cleared her throat, finally reining in her thoughts. "You have a date with Mark this afternoon."

Between her disastrous date with Nilesh and this morning, Abigail had wavered what felt like a million times. Her mind ping-ponged back and forth between defeat and determination. It had been an exhausting few days. Abigail felt a queasiness in her stomach at the thought of this afternoon's date with Mr. Rivera. She couldn't decide if it was a good or bad queasiness, maybe both.

"Mark Rivera, wasn't he..." Abigail hesitated, recalling fragments of conversations past.

"Yep, just a fling," Tessa confirmed, dismissing the thought with a wave. "But enough about my ancient history."

"Well, it might be your ancient history, but it is my present and future. Details would help." Abigail was not letting her off the hook that easily. While Tessa was notorious for her epically brief relationships, nearly all had a reason the relationship ended. Tessa gravitated to trouble.

"Ugh, fine. Mark is a successful entrepreneur, self-assured, average conversationalist, and good to great in the sac." Tessa read off with the same level of emotion she would have reading out his resume.

"Mark doesn't have whatever made Terrance worthy of being a 'Three-date-Terrance," Abigail teased. "So, if past flings are on the table, why aren't you setting me up with Terrance? He was the best of the bunch?"

Tessa let out an exaggerated sigh, not thrilled to have to explain her reason. "There is no 'Three-date-Terrance'. He graduated to 'Five-date-Terrance', and I think I may stop counting and call him Terrance," vulnerability creeping into her voice. "Before you get excited, Terrance knows I am still seeing other people, but if there were someone worth giving that up, it would be him." Abigail's jaw fell open in a double bombshell before 9 AM, and words escaped her. It had to be ten years since Tessa had a connection beyond a couple of nights.

"But let's focus on your afternoon. Are you ready for blind date round two featuring Mr. Rivera?"

"Not in the slightest," Abigail replied, her words steady but her heart fluttering like a caged bird at the prospect of another blind date orchestrated by her well-meaning but occasionally misguided best friend. Thinking about the date made her stomach churn. Perhaps she should have opted for a chamomile and peppermint blend of tea.

"Good," Tessa said, her tone shifting back to its usual confident timbre. "But, just in case, I lined up another date tomorrow night. Details to follow." Tessa rushed, jumping from her chair and running off before Abigail could respond.

"What?" Abigail's question was left dangling in the air.

Abigail sat perched on a high bar stool. She had opted for a short-sleeve dress to avoid any sleeves dipping into drinks. The sounds of drafts being poured provided a comforting backdrop to her nervous anticipation—it sounded like sheets or rain slapping the pavement. For the umpteenth time since arriving, Abigail repeated an inspiring mantra: "I am strong and worthy."

The bar was alive with patron chatter and the clinking of glasses, an aromatic blend of hops and malt hanging thick in the air. The room's energy was more electric compared to the café shop. A new location for a new date.

As with her date with Nilesh, Abigail asked Jules to go silent so she could focus on the person she was to interact with.

"Abigail Sorensen?" a confident voice rang out over the din, and she turned toward the source.

"Hi, Mark?" Abigail greeted, extending a hand that he clasped firmly in his own.

"The one and only," Mark replied with self-assurance. A direct contrast to the anxiousness Nilesh had exuded.

Mark took his seat, using one hand to guide him, the other still holding Abigail's. He ordered them both pints and returned his attention back to her. At no point did he ever release her hand. Abigail tried to remember other dates before Ryker. She remembered some were more handsy than others, but that was not usually her hand they were trying to touch. His grip remained loose, and she decided to wait for an appropriate time to break the connection.

As the server slid their two drinks onto the tabletop, Abigail took the opportunity to twist and pull her hand away. She occupied both hands by encircling them around the cold glass.

"I ordered us both a pale ale from a local microbrewery. The owner and I go way back. I am sure you will enjoy it." Mark's confidence seemed to leave no room for Abigail to disagree. Wouldn't someone usually say, 'I hope you will enjoy it' instead of 'I know you will,' Abigail wondered.

Abigail took a small sip, cautious not to gag if it was terrible. It was okay, not the best in the world, but it wasn't skunky either. Abigail was partial to stouts with a creamy caramel undertone.

"Great, right," Mark stated.

Abigail clenched her teeth at his tone. Feeling obligated to compliment his choice but also express her own opinion. "I guess for a pale ale, it is good."

"Great, I'll let my friend you enjoyed it. I knew you

would." Mark had heard something different in Abigail's response than what she intended.

Abigail didn't want Mark to order her another drink. She took small sips and returned the glass to the table, one hand moving to cover the opening. Instinct told her to nurse the beer and protect herself. Mark would not regain control of her drink.

"So, you teach at the same high school as Tessa." Again, a statement, not a question. Mark's fingers brushed over her, the back of her hand still clenching the pint of beer.

Abigail took a small sip of beer, forcing his fingers away, but they settled back on her hand when her glass returned to the table's surface. It would be counterproductive if she kept using drinking her beer as a strategy to keep his hands away. The beer would vanish rapidly.

"Tessa says you are an entrepreneur. What line of work would that be?" Abigail asked, modeling how a conversation should work. Mark's fingers felt rough and maybe calloused. Abigail was unsure what type of entrepreneurial work would leave his fingers so worn.

"Oh, this and that. I diversify my investments into different channels to keep things interesting." Abigail could hear Mark's hands flapping in the air as he spoke, but at least it was a momentary reprieve from his touch. His response seemed unspecific and lacked an air of honesty.

Before Abigail could reply, Mark pushed his fingers between her hand and the glass, forcing Abigail to release the beer. With her hand no longer secure, Mark grabbed it back tightly.

Mark pulled her hand up while pushing towards her in what felt like a rehearsed move. The action forced Abigail to bend her elbow or be pushed back off her stool. With her elbow bent, Mark could push his forearm against hers and lean in.

"Your skin is incredibly smooth," Abigail cringed as Mark's attempt at a seductive tone came out scratchy and obscene.

Abigail tried to extricate herself from his grip, grimacing in discomfort. "Uh, thanks," she said, more out of habit than accepting the compliment. She didn't care about Mark's opinion.

"I am partial to physical connections. I believe a simple touch can communicate so much." With his free hand, he traced the outline of Abigail's arm, tentative at first, but the pressure increased with each passing nanosecond.

Abigail winced as his fingers dug into her upper arm. Abigail thought Tessa's 'good feeling' radar must be broken. This interaction was not a pleasant feeling.

"Your hands are so soft," Mark continued, oblivious to her discomfort. "What you can tell from just a simple touch is amazing."

"Is it?" Abigail questioned lightly, though her mind was already racing for an escape plan. She subtly shifted in her seat, distancing herself from his probing hands.

"Absolutely," he insisted. Abigail could hear him moving her drink away. She assumed to either take her other hand or, worse, drug her drink.

Before he had a chance, Abigail motioned her hand to her ear, tapping for Jules three times. "Abigail," a savior's voice chirped in her ear. "To confirm you are at risk, please clear your throat. If it was an accident, advise or tap the earpiece again." Jules's calming tone instructed.

Without hesitation, Abigail cleared her throat, thankful for the AI's help. A pre-established alert, Abigail had programmed reactivated Jules while silently notifying him of her distress.

"Driverless car en route. Your tab has been paid. I will signal you when the car arrives. Stay strong," came the swift response. Relief washed over Abigail, knowing she wasn't alone. Abigail knew without a doubt that if she whispered to Jules, she could not wait. Every other AI in the bar would be immediately notified of her distress, urging strangers to intercede. Abigail was so moved she wanted to cry, but would not give Mark any sign that she was not in control.

"Car is pulling up to the door now. Time to leave," Jules instructed.

"Mark, something's come up," Abigail announced without apology. Mark was reluctant to release her arm, and standing and forcing the separation hurt. With an assertive jerk, she was able to stand upright. "I have to go."

"Wait, we're just getting started," he protested, grabbing her arm again.

The unresolved fury she felt for the man who had attacked her years ago collided with her anger tonight—venomous rage boiled in Abigail's gut. "Let go of me," she spat, punctuating each word for emphasis. The command must have shocked Mark enough that his hand loosened. Abigail took advantage of the slip without losing a beat and twisted her arm around, breaking his hold. Without pause, she headed out the door directly into the waiting car, Jules and the feedback sensors guiding her purposeful steps.

Abigail slid into the car, her body still vibrating with irritation. She took a few breaths to calm the rage as the car rolled away from the bar effortlessly. Briefly, she contemplated crying to release her pent-up anger. But the tears did not come; instead, a sense of empowerment washed over her. She had stood up for herself, set firm boundaries, and asserted control in an uncomfortable situation. Tonight, she was her hero.

Chapter 11

"Abigail, it's not even six in the morning. What's got you up and dialing?" Tessa's voice crackled with sleep as she answered the call.

"Last night's date with Mark was a disaster, Tess. I can't go through that again," Abigail said, her fingers tracing the edge of her coffee mug, the ceramic cool against her skin. Her mind still carried the weight of Mark's intrusive touches, the memory etched into her nerves like a sour aftertaste.

"What happened?" Tessa asked, now alert with concern.

"I needed Jules's help to rescue me before Mark's relentless grip broke an arm. The man seemed to think he was entitled to overpower me." Abigail took a deep breath after sharing the lowlights with Tessa before she backed out.

"Oh, honey, I am so sorry. You know, not that I think about it, that Mark was a little handsy," Tessa admitted apologetically. "Maybe it was Mark with a 'c' that was the fun night out." The realization dawned upon her.

"Tess, you know I love you, but you are a terrible matchmaker. You can't even remember who you are setting me up with. Perhaps it slipped your mind that tonight's date might be a serial killer, and I could end up as his next victim?" Abigail's voice hitched, frustration and vulnerability lacing her words. She knew she was overreacting, but her gut twisted with panic. Abigail started moving back and forth in her living room like a trapped creature, anxiety bubbling at the surface.

Tessa sighed, the sound heavy with empathy. "Levi is different, trust me. And hey, didn't you say we should keep trying new experiences?"

Abigail paused mid-pace, her hand resting on the back of a chair. She knew Tessa meant well, but her heart still hammered from last night's ordeal. "Experience doesn't mean repeating mistakes, Tess. My gut says this is a bad idea."

"Your gut also said you'd never enjoy sushi, and look at you now," Tessa scoffed in a light tone, trying to bring a smile to Abigail's lips, even if she couldn't see it.

"Fine, but sushi didn't leave permanent indentations in my arms," Abigail shot back, unwilling to ease the tension.

"Okay, I'll give you that one," Tessa conceded, her bed creaking as she presumably got up. "But seriously, Abigail, Levi's a sweetheart. You've got my word."

Abigail took a long breath. "What makes Levi different? Did he warrant two dates? Maybe he saved a litter of puppies from a rabid coyote?" Abigail knew she was grasping at straws, but the situation seemed absurd.

"Full disclosure now, Abi, I have never been involved with Levi, nor would I ever. Not because there is something wrong with him, but because he is my brother's best friend, and making out with him would be like kissing a brother. As for the litter of puppies, I don't recall any stories like that, but if there were a litter of puppies in peril, Levi would do his best to rescue them." Tessa's voice lacked sarcasm or humor. This was raw, honest Tessa.

Abigail knew the feeling of defeat; her shoulders slumped, and she let out an exhausted yawn. Tessa's description of Levi painted him in a gentle light, a stark contrast to the discomfort of her date with Mark. The warmth in Tessa's voice was evidence enough of her belief in Levi's character, and it tipped the scales in his favor.

"Okay, okay," Abigail capitulated. "But you have to come with me—for moral support and bodyguard if I need it."

"Third-wheeling it on your date? That's my specialty." Sarcastic Tessa had returned in full force.

"Please, Tess. I don't think I can do this if you aren't there," Abigail pleaded.

"I won't go on your date with you, but I will bring Terrance—not as a double date," Tessa added before Abigail could squeal about a double take with the famous Terrance. "Terrance and I will sit at another table, just in case." Tessa compromised.

"Deal," Abigail agreed, relief washing over her. Tessa's presence bolstered her, even if it was just a safety net.

"You know, if the date goes bad, I can join the two of you and interrogate the 'multi-date Terrance," Abigail teased.

"Don't you dare!" Tessa's response is part serious, part humor. "Now, leave me alone. I can still get 45 minutes of sleep before I need to get ready for work."

"K, talk to you soon. I could have waited until our morning café run," Abigail apologized.

"Ya think?" Tessa replied before disconnecting the call.

"Positive thinking, Abigail," she said aloud to herself. Your school day will be productive. You will come home and get ready for this date, spilling nothing. "You will have a wonderful date." Perhaps if she repeated the mantra a hundred more times, she could manifest it to happen.

Abigail stood before her wardrobe, the smooth wood familiar under her fingertips. Her arms ached—a sad reminder of Mark's overbearing grip from the night before. As she ran her hands over the sleeves of various outfits, she winced at the tender spots where his fingers had pressed too firmly.

"Jules," Abigail called out softly, her voice tinged with vulnerability, "are there bruises?"

"Abigail," Jules responded in a tone that conveyed concern despite its digital origin, "While I may not see signs of bruising, it is evident that pain lingers both on the surface and beneath it. Physical or not, your discomfort is valid and warrants care."

A small, grateful smile graced Abigail's lip. It was uncanny how comforting an AI could be. "Thank you, Jules," she whispered, her heart swelling with appreciation for the technology that had become her steadfast companion.

She chose a thick-sleeved sweater, its fabric soft yet substantial enough to provide a sense of security. Levi couldn't see the marks—only Jules and the world's AI could—but that wasn't the point. The sweater felt like armor, a protective layer between herself and the world, between yesterday's mistakes and today's possibilities.

"Does this look okay?" Abigail asked, though she knew Jules's programming was more practical than fashion. He would let her know if she completely missed the mark.

"According to current style algorithms, your choice is chic and suitable for the occasion," Jules assured her. "More importantly, if it makes you feel safe and comfortable, it is perfect."

"Thanks, Jules," she said, her heart lighter. She took a deep breath, inhaling the faint lavender scent of her perfume—a small sensory pleasure before stepping out into the unpredictable evening.

"Remember, Abigail," Jules chimed in one last time as she prepared to leave, "no matter what transpires tonight, your experiences are yours to savor, learn from, and above all, they should bring you joy."

"Joy," Abigail repeated, the word hanging in the air like a promise. "Jules, tonight I will leave you activated for the date." With that, she tucked the lingering doubts away, wrapped the comfort of her sweater closer, and stepped out the door, ready to meet whatever melody life would play next.

Abigail's cane tapped rhythmically against the pavement as she approached the Tex-Mex restaurant; lively music serenaded the evening air. It was a beautiful evening for a walk, the air welt crisp and a subtle breeze felt refreshing against her skin. Abigail collapsed her cane now that she was in a congested area, relying on Jules for direction.

The clinking of silverware and laughter seeped through the walls, mingling with the twang of a steel guitar drifting on the breeze. As she crossed the threshold, the aroma of sizzling fajitas and spicy salsa hit her, enveloping her in a warm, piquant hug.

"Welcome to El Corazón," a cheerful hostess greeted. "How may I assist you?"

"Thank you. I'm meeting someone, Levi?" Abigail replied, her voice steady, betraying none of the butterflies dancing in her stomach.

"Of course! Right this way."

The restaurant hummed with life. An eclectic assortment of instruments played lively country music from integrated speakers, filling the space with an exuberance of energy that made Abigail's toes tap involuntarily.

"Your table," the host said, guiding Abigail to her seat.

"Levi was here; he must have stepped away, but I am sure he will be back any minute now."

"Thank you. Do you know Levi?" Her tone denoted a certain familiarity when she said his name.

"Oh yes, dear, Levi is here almost every night. He is probably off chatting up an employee or other regulars. He is quite the social butterfly. So charming." The host had a strong Southern accent. Abigail wondered if that was part of her work persona or authentic. "Is there anything I can ask a server to bring while you wait, honey?" The woman's easy familiarity was endearing. Whether it was an act or genuine didn't matter.

"I am all right, thank you. I'll wait until Levi returns." Abigail settled into her seat and began tracing the surface of the textured tabletop. Her fingers brush over the embossed pattern of stars and horseshoes. How very quaint.

She didn't have to wait long. Within moments, confident footsteps approached from the opposite direction.

"Abigail? Hi, I'm Levi Mason," came the rich and melodic greeting. His voice could coax a smile from even the most guarded heart.

"Hello, Levi," Abigail responded, turning towards him. His presence was magnetic, his personality already permeating the space between them.

"Sorry, am I late?" he asked, pulling out a chair with a smooth scrape against the floor. "I hope you haven't been waiting long."

"Not at all," Abigail assured him. "I just arrived myself."

"Great!" Levi exclaimed, his tone light and playful. "I've been looking forward to this all day. There's nothing like Mexican food to spark pleasant conversation, right?"

"Or at least a mutual appreciation for guacamole," Abigail joked, an awkward chortle escaping her lips. The chuckle was more nerves than humor. She felt a tad embarrassed; it wasn't a suitable response and was not at all funny.

"Ah, a fellow guac enthusiast!" Levi laughed, clearly delighted. "They say you can tell a lot about a person by how they treat their chips and salsa.' Abigail felt redeemed that Levi could respond to her guacamole comment. At least the date wasn't over before it started.

"Is that so?" Abigail tilted her head, enjoying the humor in his words. "And what does it say if I admit to being a serial double-dipper?"

"Bold," Levi leaned in conspiratorially, "and unafraid to take risks. I like that."

A smile spread across Abigail's face, reaching her eyes and lifting the weight that had been crushing on her for days. She hadn't felt such a genuine, carefree smile in ages. Levi's charm was infectious, and his friendly demeanor put her at ease. There was something refreshingly candid about him, a sense of openness that invited trust.

"Tell me, Levi," Abigail said, leaning forward, her curiosity piqued. "What's your story? Every musician has one."

"Ah, my story." He exhaled a breathy sound and then took a deep breath as if he were going to recite a long epic tale. Anticipating amusement, Abigail readied herself. "It's a bit country, a bit rock 'n' roll, and a lot of chasing dreams. But tonight, it's all about getting to know you, Abigail Sorensen." Well, that was a tad disappointing. Abigail settled in for a long story, not expecting the conversation ball to be tossed back so soon.

"I am pretty average. I can't even say what genre of music my story would be. Elevator music, perhaps." A note of sadness infused in her tone. Did she consider herself that generic? She had a zest for life, followed by setbacks, and was now foraging a fresh path. Maybe she was more Vivaldi's Four Seasons. Rumination for another day. She needed to focus back on this blind date.

Jules' gentle, artificial voice broke through her thoughts. "Abigail, Tessa has arrived with a companion. It is likely her date."

"Thank you, Jules," Abigail responded, the artificial intelligence's timely updates never ceasing to amaze her. While Levi's presence was easygoing, knowing Tessa was now in the building gave Abigail a comforting sense of security.

Levi's voice held worry as he asked, "Are you all right?"

"Everything is fine," she replied confidently. "My friend just walked in." Abigail relaxed her hands on the table, feeling the knots in her stomach loosen at the thought of Tessa's lively presence.

"Your friend? Would that be our mutual acquaintance? It must be reassuring to have your crew watching out for you."

"Yes, it is nice to feel the support. I'm sure you have some interesting stories about our shared acquaintance. Maybe we can exchange some tales," Abigail suggested.

"I'm not so sure about that. Not that I don't have my fair share of crazy stories! But Tessa can be pretty intimidating when she feels ganged up on," Levi spoke with obvious affection for his pseudo-sister.

Abigail shook her head. "I don't know about that. Feed Tessa some tasty morsels, and she is putty in your hands."

"Ah, that's right. You are the one with the magic culinary skills. Unfortunately, food is not my specialty. While Tessa may not bite the hand that feeds her, she has no problem turning on the boy that helped her brother tease her." Levi responded. "My talent, while it should lull a hydra to sleep, has no impact on our fair, Tessa."

"What is your talent? I assume it is not playing a harp?" Abigail replied, imagining Tessa with three heads, each biting at anyone who got too close.

"I am a singer who performs here from 9 PM until they kick us out or we run out of songs—whichever comes first. No harp in the band."

"I guess this is not a harp-type ambiance. I assume this clientele is more soft rock, country, or blended country rock. Am I close?"

"Nailed it. It depends on the night. I understand the diners' energy and will move across the rock-country spectrum. However, my preferences lean toward country music." Levi was proud of his path and continued, "Music's my life. There's just something about storytelling through song that gets me."

"Country music has a way of searing stories into the heart," Abigail acknowledged, tapping her fingers rhythmically on the table.

"Exactly!" Levi exclaimed, his enthusiasm palpable. "So, if you stick around, you'll get a front-row seat to the Levi Mason Experience."

"Sounds tempting," she said, genuinely considering it. She could already imagine the strings of his guitar vibrating with life, the warm timbre of authentic country music filling the space.

As the sounds of the Tex-Mex restaurant continued to swirl around them, Abigail felt a newfound appreciation for the unexpected twists life could offer. Every moment, she grew more captivated by the man opposite her—a musician with an irresistible charisma and a mysterious voice.

"You must be pretty confident to perform on stage every night. Don't you feel...judged?" Abigail asked, voicing her insecurities.

"Not really, maybe in the beginning. But once you realize you can't please everyone and go for it, the power of judgment from others diminishes," he reassured her genuinely. "I was more nervous about meeting you today."

"Really?" She found comfort in his honesty. "You hide it well."

"Years of performing on stage have taught me how to keep a poker face," he chuckled. "But beneath this calm exterior is a man who knocked over his water glass before you arrived. I went to change into a fresh shirt from my performance bag."

Abigail let out a deep rolling guffaw, not holding back the belly laugh that reverberated across her body. She had her fair share of clumsiness the last week, especially with liquids. "Well, we're in good company, then. I almost walked into a cactus on my way in."

"Ah, a poor decorative choice in the main corridor. The cactus dance occurs often, a rite of passage around here."

"I guess I'm fitting right in," Abigail smiled, feeling a connection forming unexpectedly.

"More than you know," Levi whispered conspiratorially. "I may or may not have had my prickly encounter when I first entered this place."

"It looks like we're meant to be comrades in arms—or should I say thorns?" Abigail's words were light, but an underlying sincerity connected them.

"Thorns it is." Levi raised his glass in a toast. "To unexpected meetings and the beauty of facing our thorns."

Their glasses clinked together, creating a crisp sound amidst the gentle clinking of silverware and soft conversations in the background. As Abigail took a deep breath, she was delighted to catch a whiff of Levi's cologne—a subtle blend of cedarwood and citrus that made her feel grounded and exhilarated. After the events of last night, it was a relief to be in the company of someone who brought her comfort instead of anxiety.

As they continued their conversation, Abigail was fully immersed in the warmth of Levi's voice and the effortless flow of their dialogue. It was a refreshing change from her previous dates, where she had felt uncomfortable and out of place. Here was a man who exuded kindness and respect, and she couldn't help but be drawn to him.

"Thank you," Abigail said sincerely. "For making this evening feel so...normal."

"Normal is underrated," Levi agreed. "Especially when it's accompanied by such excellent company."

"Cheers to normalcy then." Abigail raised her glass once more.

"Cheers," Levi echoed, meeting her glass with his own in a toast that solidified their newfound friendship.

At that moment, Abigail realized that sharing a meal with someone who respected her boundaries was a rare gift she would never take for granted.

"Abigail," he said casually, his tone inviting, "would you mind if I played my guitar for a bit? To warm up before my set tonight?"

"I would love to hear you play," Abigail replied with genuine curiosity.

Levi retrieved his guitar from beside his chair—an instrument that seemed like an extension of himself. His fingers glided over the strings, producing a series of mellow, harmonious chords that filled the space between them like velvet.

As Levi hummed, the mood in the room shifted unexpectedly. Abigail was caught off guard by the sound. It wasn't the deep, resonant hum she had expected, but something entirely different. It was pitchy and erratic, leaving her perplexed.

"Is this a new piece you're working on?" she asked politely, trying to mask her bewilderment.

"Just something I've been experimenting with," Levi replied, unaware of Abigail's inner turmoil.

As he sang small lyrics, Abigail's confusion only deepened. The charming voice that had captivated her moments ago now sounded more like cats meowing—grating, discordant, and unpleasant. It was like biting into orange segments but getting a lemon instead.

"Very... unique," she managed, struggling to find the right words between politeness and honesty.

"Thanks! I'm all about pushing boundaries with my music," Levi responded enthusiastically, oblivious to how his singing made her cringe internally.

Abigail could feel the discomfort crawling up her spine, like the repulsion she felt when someone chewed with their mouth open near her—an intimate yet unwelcome sensory experience.

"Yes, definitely boundary-pushing," Abigail echoed with forced cheerfulness. She tightened her grip on her glass, using the firm surface as an anchor while navigating through the dissonance of the moment.

Her mind raced as she struggled to reconcile Levi's magnetic personality with the auditory nightmare unfolding before her. His off-key warbling was now smothering the initial attraction ignited by his charm and wit.

"Would you like another drink?" Levi asked, interrupting her thoughts.

"Levi," Abigail spoke firmly as she set down her glass. "I think I should call it a night," the words said before Abigail had thought it through. Did she want to end the evening? Within seconds, Abigail played out her emotions in her head. So, he's a lousy singer. He doesn't smell and doesn't physically hurt me. But music is a massive part of his life. She couldn't lie forever. How would she feel if someone said they loved her cooking but were secretly spitting in their napkin? She doesn't want to be with that person, and neither should Levi. Okay, she was good with her decision. After several seconds of internal debate, Abigail relaxed, confident of her unexpected choice to end the date early.

"Already?" His voice showed genuine disappointment—a contrast to the discordance of his singing. "I was hoping we could chat some more after my set."

Abigail's heart sank at the disappointment in his voice, a stark contrast to the discordant notes of his singing. She hoped to spare his feelings as she mustered a softness in her tone. "You're incredibly kind, and I've enjoyed our conversation, but I'm just not feeling the connection I was hoping for."

"I thought we were connecting well until I started my warm-up. Do you not like my singing?" Hurt echoed in his question.

"It's not just the music," Abigail admitted gently, trying to find the right words. "It's... complicated. You're lovely, Levi. Truly. But I am on my personal journey right now, and it requires me to go with my gut or intuition. It might not seem logical all the time, but my instincts say I am not the person to join your entourage." It was true. Her instincts had called it quits before her brain could agree. She may kick herself later for walking away from such a nice man, but she had picked a path.

"Fair enough," he said, though the crestfallen drop in his voice tugged at her heartstrings. "I appreciate your candor."

"Thank you for understanding," Abigail said, standing up from the table. Her need to exit gracefully tempered the desire to flee the scene.

Levi took a moment before responding, the gracious light returning to his voice. "Take care, Abigail." As she walked away, Abigail couldn't help but feel a sense of melancholy, knowing that their brief encounter would amount to nothing now.

Abigail navigated her way through the restaurant, guided by Jules and the sound of Tessa's voice. She approached Tessa's table, the smell of flowers and laughter signaling she was close.

"Abigail!" Tessa's voice came warmly as she noticed her friend's approach.

"Hey, Tess," Abigail greeted Tessa.

"Come meet Terrance," Tessa said, her excitement palpable.

"Nice to meet you, Abigail," came a smooth voice that vibrated with genuine friendliness.

"Terrance, a pleasure," Abigail replied, extending a hand, which he shook quickly. Tessa's contented sigh filled the space between them, and Abigail could almost feel the radiance of her friend's happiness. It had been too long since she'd heard such lightness in Tessa's tone.

"Everything okay with your date?" Tessa asked, a hint of concern threading her words.

Abigail shrugged lightly, folding her hands in front of her. "Levi is nice. Nice-" she started, feeling her way through the explanation. "But we just didn't click, you know? I think it's more me than him."

"Ah, that's too bad. He seemed like a catch," Tessa said.

"He is," Abigail confessed, holding back the truth of Levi's less-than-stellar vocal performance. "Sometimes the notes just don't harmonize, no matter how much you want them to."

"Fair enough," Tessa said, her curiosity stirred but appreciating Abigail's privacy for once. "You'll find someone who sings your tune soon enough."

"Thanks, Tess. I'm glad you've found someone who seems to make you so happy," Abigail said, the warmth in her heart outweighing the bittersweet tang of her unsuccessful evening.

"Me too," Tessa's voice beamed.

"Enjoy the rest of your night, you two," Abigail offered, already turning to leave.

"Text me later?" Tessa called after her.

"Will do," Abigail promised, her footsteps light as she exited into the cool embrace of the night, leaving the cacophony of the Tex-Mex haven behind her.

Abigail sat reclined on her plush sofa in her apartment's quiet sanctuary. The stillness was a stark contrast to the evening's discordant serenade. She couldn't help but laugh as she mentally replayed the scenes from her recent attempts at finding romance. With each silent giggle, the absurdity of her dating life seemed to unravel before her.

"First, there was Nilesh," she mused, scrunching her nose at the memory of his overpowering atomizers mingled with the mustiness of deceit. "Smell and dishonesty—what a combination." Her fingers absentmindedly traced embossed patterns on the armrest.

"Then Mark," she continued, shivering at the ghost of his intrusive hands. "Touch that went from bold to unbearable in less time than it takes to hail an auto cab." She rubbed her arms as if to erase the sensation that had lingered far longer than it was welcome.

"And tonight," Abigail sighed, pressing the heels of her palms against her eyes as Levi's off-key warbling bounced around her skull. "Sound has officially joined the ranks of sensory saboteurs." A peal of laughter escaped her lips, bubbling up from the depths of her diaphragm. Her failed dates were checking off a list of repulsions, one sense at a time.

"Good grief, if I go on another date, it'll probably implode because of taste. What could go wrong? Kissing a man who eats onions like apples?" she snorted, imagining the ludicrous scenario. With her luck, it would be far worse.

Collecting herself, Abigail reached for her smart device and started a group message with Tessa and Imani. Her fingers danced across the braille display with practiced ease. "Hey, lovelies. I just wanted to say I love you both. Your matchmaking skills are... unique," she typed, a wry smile stretching across her lips.

"Appreciate all the setups, but I think I'm going to sit out the next few rounds of blind-date-bingo," she added, hitting send before she could second-guess her commitment.

There was a beat of silence before her device vibrated with incoming replies. "Blind-date-bingo, I could make a drinking game of that. Come on, let's play some more." The computerized voice did not capture Tessa's joie de vie.

"You are sure, Abigail? You know it takes a minimum of four rounds to win at bingo. The fourth or fifth time might be the charm!" Imani's text read, her optimism shining through even in digital form.

"I am a thousand percent sure. Besides, there's always Club Ke Kino if I need a little excitement," Abigail wrote back, her words laced with humor and a dash of mischief.

"Wait, what happened at Club Ke Kino?!" Tessa's response instantly came through, and her curiosity was practically audible.

Abigail let out a soft giggle, placing the device down. She didn't need to see Tessa's perplexed expression to feel the itch of her friend's prying mind. She chose the sweet satisfaction of keeping her escapades under wraps tonight, letting Tessa stew in the mystery a little longer.

As her laughter died down, Abigail reclined further into the cushions, her thoughts drifting to the sensory chaos that had become her love life. Yet, even amidst the misadventures, her spirit remained unbroken. If anything, her soul was more vibrant and self-assured.

"Club Ke Kino," she murmured. Warmth radiated across her body at the memory. Abigail chewed at her lip, remembering the sensations. How safe and unfettered she had been. Among her recent outings, it was the best.

Chapter 12

The entrancing bouquet of freshly brewed coffee merged with the warm, buttery aroma of croissants diffusing into every corner of Abigail's apartment—a sensory invitation that made the space feel like a cozy Parisian café. The gentle hum of music played in the background, complementing the symphony of city sounds that seeped in from the open window. Amidst this tranquil setting, the unexpected tap of the door knocker chimed in.

"Coming!" Abigail called out as she navigated toward the entrance with practiced ease. She could tell by the rhythm of the knock that it was Imani—no one else had quite the same predictability. A snap of knock, pause, two quick knocks, pause, one last knock. Abigail wondered why Imani never used the integrated doorbell; it would have been more efficient, a characteristic she associated with Imani.

"Abigail," Imani announced as the door swung open, her

voice bubbling enthusiastically. "You will not believe what I've stumbled upon."

"Good morning to you, too. As for what you stumbled on, it could range from a new subatomic particle to a two-for-one sale on those dark chocolates we love." Abigail stepped aside, her hands reaching out, and she found Imani's arms to guide her inside.

"Ha! Your taste buds are spot-on, but today is about matters of the heart," Imani said in an enthusiastic sing-song manner. Abigail led Imani to her favorite armchair. The tactile familiarity of the woven fabric she traced added comfort to the visit.

"Is that so?" Abigail mused and returned to her kitchen to pour another cup of coffee. The liquid's warmth spread through the ceramic mug, a welcome contrast to the coolness of the countertop. "I thought we agreed—no more setups for a while. My blind date bingo card is on pause." This conversation warranted cookies, Abigail thought, grabbing a container from the fridge and tucking it under her arm.

"Ah, but that was before I heard about this one. This isn't just any setup, Abigail. While I prefer to rely on scientific data to make conclusions, this one is serendipitous!" Imani's tone buzzed with infectious optimism, an exuberant trait few people have had the pleasure to witness in Imani.

"Serendipity?" Abigail balanced the two mugs, her fingers deftly avoiding the steam rising in wispy tendrils. She returned to the living room, offering one to Imani with a knowing chuckle. "A fluke doesn't sound reassuring as a basis to meet with another stranger."

Imani accepted the mug, the hint of a giggle in her throat. "I wouldn't say fluke, more fortunate coincidence, or the stars aligning in your favor." For a woman who leverages scientific principles in most decisions, the 'stars aligning' was out of character.

"The stars, as in enormous balls of toxic gas that will eventually explode and form a black hole?" Abigail replied, sinking into the couch opposite Imani. The cushions embraced her, familiar and comforting. A sip of her coffee was rich and robust, grounding her amidst the whirling excitement that Imani radiated. "Who are you, and what have you done with Imani?" Abigail jested.

"Stop being such a pessimist. I know the record has been bad, but habes multam ranarum basia ut princeps tuus." The shift to Latin indicated Imani's increased level of excitement.

"Just because I teach biology doesn't mean I speak Latin. I got 'frogs' from 'ranarum'. Not a good start, Imani."

"You need to kiss many frogs to find your prince. Come on, Abigail, hear me out," Imani begged.

"All right, then. Tell me about this mysterious frog."

"Let's just say he comes highly recommended by a friend of a friend. And..." Imani leaned forward, eager to spill the beans yet holding back enough for the mystery, "...he's been told quite a bit about you, too—only the best, of course."

"Of course," Abigail echoed, dripping with sarcasm. Unsure of what to say next, Abigail opened the container of cookies as a distraction.

"Think of it as an adventure," Imani urged, sensing her friend's hesitation. "Sometimes life defies plans and analysis. Sometimes, you must taste the unpredictable."

"True," Abigail conceded, her mind wandering to the unsavory possibilities. "But I reserve the right to spit it out if it tastes funny." The omen of date number four succumbing to taste rearing its head.

"Deal," Imani agreed, her laughter filling the room like sunshine breaking through clouds, unaware of the foreboding in Abigail's mind. "Speaking of taste, I smell rosemary. Are those cookies you have yet to offer me?"

"You know your herbs. These are my rosemary and lemon melts. They melt fast, so don't dunk them in your coffee." Abigail reached out the box and tapped on the side of Imani's chair to show the location. Imani grabbed two, popping the first in her mouth.

"I believe you have mastered the recipe. This should be the first recipe you publish." Imani plopped the second in her mouth. "I know what you can get me for my birthday."

"Flattery won't get me to agree to your plotting." Abigail grabbed her cookie and let it dissolve against her tongue. It felt like an infusion of flavors directly absorbed by her sensory system. "However, if a date tasted like this, I would be hooked."

Imani took a few sips of her coffee and remained silent, as if she had forgotten why she was there. The power of a good cookie. Abigail gave her friend a moment before pressing forward. "So, a friend-of-a-friend, do I know this friend-of-a-friend recommending this match?"

Before continuing, Imani took another long sip of her coffee. "You know both friends. I am, of course, friend number one, and friend number two is...Nilesh."

"Imani, I only know one Nilesh." Abigail was growing wary of another blind date and let out a soft growl in frustration. "If you remember, my date with Nilesh did not go well. What makes you think he has the answers to my love life?" Steam grew in Abigail's voice, recalling the fiasco of a date with her nose twitching in pain.

Oblivious to Abigail's tone and trepidation, Imani replied, "Yep, that's the friend. He was filled with remorse regarding your situation. He insists you deserve someone amazing and thinks he knows just the guy."

Abigail arched an eyebrow, unseen but implied in her tone. "Does he now? And Nilesh's matchmaking skills are...?"

"Untested. But it must be better than his blind date skills," Imani said with a diplomatic snicker. "The man in question isn't just some random suggestion. Nilesh collaborates with him at the police department."

"Ah, and when did anxious Nilesh become a police officer?"

"No, silly, Nilesh isn't a police officer; he works as a consultant technician. Detective Malik Callahan works at the police department. They've known each other for years."

"Detective, huh?" She imagined someone as meek as

Nilesh making it through the ranks to become a detective, and the idea was hard to reconcile.

"Nilesh speaks highly of him," Imani continued. "Says he's the kindest man on the planet, which is saying something given that Nilesh gets anxious around everyone, but with Detective Callahan, it's different. Even Nilesh feels at ease with him."

"Kindness is a rare and undervalued trait," Abigail noted, her interest piqued despite herself. It was hard to resist Imani's enthusiasm.

"Exactly!" Imani said, sensing the shift in Abigail's demeanor. "And kindness is just the tip of the iceberg. According to Nilesh, Malik is wise, intelligent, and funny. He could make a joke about DNA sequencing and have the entire room in stitches." There was no question Nilesh appreciated the detective's intelligence.

"DNA sequencing humor, my favorite," Abigail joked, the smile reaching her voice. It was easy to laugh with Imani, to let go of reservations, and imagine the potential of a blind date that wouldn't end in disaster. Or perhaps the humor was that she knew it would end in disaster but would likely go on this date despite that. It's not as if her friends steamroll her into these dates. It is more the infectious nature of their enthusiasm.

"Then it's settled! You'll meet him," Imani declared triumphantly.

"Whoa there, I didn't say—"

"Come on, Abigail. You can't tell me you're not even curious."

"Fine," Abigail relented, shaking her head in mock exasperation while secretly allowing the seed of excitement to grow. "Curiosity may have killed the cat, but at least it died knowing." Hopefully, one more date wouldn't kill her. Being honest with herself, she enjoyed the dates thus far, even though they didn't end in a happily ever after. At least she wasn't at home alone.

"Brilliant!" Imani clapped her hands together. "I'll let Nilesh know. But Malik agreed to meet you on Saturday - at 10 AM at the Museum of Natural History and Civilization."

The Museum was a thoughtful choice; its wide-open spaces were comforting, and the echoes of footsteps and distant conversations painted an auditory picture. It had been a few years since Abigail had accompanied a school trip to the museum. She had spent so much time tracking wayward teens that she could not explore it herself. Even if the date fails, she can still delight in the museum.

"Saturday," Abigail reflected aloud. With Imani's infectious enthusiasm as a catalyst, Abigail's anticipation bubbled up, mingling with fear. But a reasonable fear reminded her she was alive and taking risks. "Okay, I will meet Detective Malik Callahan on Saturday."

Imani savored every drop of her coffee and two more cookies before pushing herself out of the chair to leave.

"Thanks for braving the urban jungle to get here, Imani," Abigail said warmly, her hand finding the doorknob. "I know you've got a million things on your plate, what with saving the world and all."

Imani's laugh was a bright chime that filled the apartment. "It's no trouble at all. And hey, what are friends for if not to push you into the arms of handsome detectives?"

Abigail couldn't help but giggle as she opened the door, the air-conditioned draft from the hallway mingling with the warm scents of her home. "Please, tell Nilesh I appreciate him playing Cupid. It's charming. I hope he finds someone who shares his love of aromachology."

"I will do that," Imani promised, stepping out into the hall. "Nilesh's heart is in the right place, even if his sense of discretion isn't."

The door closed with a gentle click, leaving Abigail in her apartment's quiet embrace. She ran her fingers along the door frame to secure the two locks, giving the door a little pull to ensure it was locked. Safe in her apartment, her thoughts meandered as she retrieved the two used cups.

"Blind date number four," she said aloud, navigating to the kitchen. Her hands brushed against the countertops, coming to rest by the kettle. She imagined the upcoming encounter. "What tasteless catastrophe awaits this time?" Abigail pondered aloud, reaching for the sugar bowl but hesitating. "Perhaps it will be salt in the sweet tea instead of sugar? The horror!"

She grinned at the absurdity of it all as she washed their two mugs. The sound of water hitting the sink and ceramic mugs was comforting. Despite the meditative state of washing dishes, Abigail could not stop her mind from drifting back to the impending date.

"Or perhaps," she continued, her tone light and teasing, "the museum's water bottle filling station will be an unwitting participant in a sewage mix-up." She cringed at the thought, shaking her head. "Only one way to find out. Malik Callahan, you better be worth it," she murmured. Whether fate would serve her sweetness or a bitter twist, Abigail Sorensen was ready to savor every moment.

Chapter 13

Abigail's fingertips traced the braille inscription at the base of the Museum of Natural History and Civilization's grand entrance sign, her pulse ticking up with every fluttering beat. The anticipation fizzled like electric champagne, sending a warm rush to her cheeks. This wasn't her first trip to the museum, but today she would not be responsible for rowdy teenagers. She wondered why she had never returned to explore the exhibits or take a friend. However, today, she would not be alone, or at least she hoped she would not.

Even this early in the morning, the sun had already warmed the air. Abigail adjusted her blouse, regretting opting for this boatneck neckline—it kept sliding off center, causing one sleeve to slip past her thumb. She had selected the top because it was billowy and breezy, carefree, and how she wanted to feel today. I guess there is some discomfort at being carefree, she thought.

"Excuse me, is this the line for the new 'Sensory Overload' exhibition?" a child's voice piped up somewhere to her right, exuberance radiating in his voice.

"No, sweetheart, that's inside," another voice replied, maternal and patient. "I'll let you know when we get there. We will head into the museum now; don't let go of my hand."

Taking her cue from the eager child, Abigail also ventured to the entrance. She wondered what the 'Sensory Overload' exhibit was about. Hopefully, it won't be as disastrous as the date with Nilesh. Abigail wanted to avoid the overwhelming sensation of overloaded olfactory senses.

The bustling sounds of the museum entrance swirled around Abigail, a symphony of life and movement. Conversations mingled like a cocktail of human emotions—excitement, curiosity, impatience—each ingredient distinct yet blending seamlessly into the auditory canvas. Footsteps echoed from the marble floor, creating a rhythm that pulsed in sync with Abigail's heart. Abigail, overwhelmed, couldn't walk and process everything. She came to a dead stop.

"Are you okay there?" A gentleman's aged voice, tinged with concern, broke through the cascade of chatter.

"Perfect, thank you," Abigail responded, aware she had stopped in his path. She could hear his walking cane tap away, retreating into the hum of museum-goers. Abigail followed the hum, letting positioning devices help navigate the simple route. She wondered if Detective Callahan had already arrived and if he was contributing to the hum of the patrons.

She inhaled deeply as she crossed the museum's threshold, a kaleidoscope of scents greeting her like an old friend. The aroma was a tapestry woven with threads of polished wood that spoke of age and care. Faint traces of paint hint at recent restorations, and an undercurrent of coffee from the museum café conjured images of crinkled newspapers and steam rising from mugs.

"Smells like history served with a side of caffeine," Abigail summarized the scents of the entrance.

"Abigail Sorensen?" The timbre of the voice that broke through the ambient murmur was deep, a sonorous note that seemed to vibrate against her skin.

"Malik Callahan, I presume?" she responded. Abigail turned in the voice's direction.

"Guilty as charged," he replied. His approaching footsteps had a confident cadence that resonated across the polished floor, announcing his presence long before they met.

Jules chirped in her ear. "Identity confirmed. Apologies for not identifying him earlier. The Police Department AIs are not accessible to public connection." The AI's self-reprimanding tone was rather comical.

"Detective," Abigail began, extending her hand, "it's a pleasure to—"

The moment their hands touched, a static shock hit them both, pulling their hands away. "Sorry," they both said in unison.

"Must be the dry air. Shall we try that again? Hi, I am

Abigail." Abigail reached out her hand, which hung in the air without a reciprocated shake.

"My apologies." Malik responded, "I was distracted for a moment," and reached for her retreating hand. Malik grasped her hand, the charge having neutralized. His grip remained loose, not what Abigail had expected from a detective. She caught a trace of citrus—sharp and sweet, like an orange popsicle on a sweltering summer day. Did the smell linger from consuming popsicles this early morning, or was he wearing the citrus scent? Abigail wondered.

"Do you have a passion for aromas, Detective?" Preparing to go their separate ways ten seconds into their date. She refused to endure another attack on her nose.

Liquid sputtered out of the Detective. He must have been midway through taking a sip. "It is Malik, not Detective. And no, unlike Nilesh, I do not have a passion for scents. My passions lie in research and detective work." His hands muffled Malik's last word as he wiped away the moisture from his drink.

"Did you research me before our meeting?" Abigail's tone took on a sharp panic note. Would he know about her attack? She had reported the crime, or rather, Jules had reported the incident. Not that she was ashamed of what happened—she was the victim. The stranger's knowledge of something undisclosed made Abigail uneasy. She wouldn't continue this date without equal footing.

"No," Malik shot back quickly. "No, I did not run a background check on you. I take my job seriously and would not abuse my access."

Moments passed in silence as they both stood, unease bubbling around them. Malik rocked back and forth on his heels rhythmically. Abigail rubbed the back of her neck, her head tilted to one side for an extra stretch. She contemplated walking away. How did things get uncomfortable so fast? She knew he was a detective before the date, but it hadn't occurred to her he might have known what had happened to her. Yes, she had perhaps challenged his integrity by asking if he had done research. Should she continue standing there in silence? Apologize? The longer the lull continued, the more awkward resuming conversation would get.

Abigail was about to ask about entering the museum when Malik spoke. "Um, we may have gotten off on the wrong foot. I assure you, Abigail, I know nothing about you. But if you are uncomfortable, we can go our separate ways, no hard feelings." Malik's voice was sincere.

"No, I am fine. I need to get out of my head. Three bad dates have left me on edge." Abigail attempted to lift her voice and smile.

"Shall we venture into the haven of history and mystery together?" Malik suggested, hesitantly offering his arm as an escort.

"Lead the way." She reached out, finding his offered arm. Her skin tingled where they touched. Not the shocking zap from before, but more of a light hum of electricity passing through them. Was the dry air of the museum to blame?

The initial unease passed. They began their first sensory

exhibit, "Gallery of the Birds." Entering the gallery, Abigail felt the size of the room; no vision was required to understand the multi-level room. Echoing sounds revealed the room's grandeur.

"It sounds beautiful," Abigail said into the ample open space. Different bird cries oscillated through the room. "These aren't just city seagulls trying to steal my muffin," Abigail said.

"It reminds me of back home. When the fields were worked, the birds all took to the sky, vocalizing their displeasure." Malik said, while speaking to the ceiling.

"Not from the city?"

"No, country born and raised. North of here, about an hour. You?" Malik inquired.

"City, this city. I left for university but couldn't wait to return home."

"Well, let's see how good you are at identifying city birds." Malik directed her to the wall. Multiple headsets lined the wall, each with a single bird call. Abigail slipped the first headset over her ears, listened, and handed it to Malik so he could hear.

"Pigeon," Abigail answered, proud she knew at least the first bird. "That cooing is one of the most distinctive bird sounds."

Malik took the second headset and listened before passing it to Abigail. He waited for her guess. "Oh, I have heard this one before. It is the one on nature programs about the Canadian wilderness, a chilling echo call. Is it the Canadian

Goose?" Abigail guessed.

"So close, a waterfowl called the common loon." Malik traced the bird's name from the braille plaque beside the headset.

"Ah, gavia immer. Do you know gavia also means joyful? It is a strange name for a bird with a haunting call."

"Do you often refer to birds by their scientific name?"

"Sometimes, they just sound better. I tell people I know a bunch of taxonomy names because I am a biology teacher, which is partly true, but I was also a nerd who memorized names to talk in 'science speak,' as my mom called it." Abigail shared.

"And how old were you when you started 'science speak'?"

"I don't know, young, four or five? It was fun."

"Oh, I am sure it was. Maybe you can teach me some more while we are here," Malik teased.

"Maybe, next bird," Abigail said, listening to more chirps and coos.

The last exhibit in the 'Bird Gallery' was an interactive comparison of wing sizes. From the 3-inch hummingbird to the nine-foot albatross, Abigail and Malik compared it to their arm span. Their conversation remained light and easy. "I can't believe we spent almost an hour in the first gallery," Abigail said as they made their way to the gallery exit.

"Yes, and technically, it is a pre-exhibit; the major museum exhibitions start in the next room. This section is used for large group meetings. I don't think I have ever found birds so interesting. Should we move on to the next section?"

As they moved farther into the cool expanse of the museum's interior, Abigail felt the artificial breeze against her skin, a stark contrast to the previous gallery that still had traces of outdoor humidity. Crossing the threshold, the AI companion earpiece nestled in her ear, automatically synchronized with the Museum AI system. A gentle voice replaced Jules, providing insight into the exhibits surrounding them.

"Welcome to the Museum of Natural History and Civilization. Please touch the displays to engage with history," the AI intoned, its cadence impersonal but as expected.

"Touch and learn, huh?" Abigail said, her fingers flexing, eager to explore. "Museums have come a long way."

"Indeed," Malik agreed. "Gone are the days of 'look but don't touch.' Now it's 'touch, hear, and sometimes even taste and smell.' Although, I think I'll pass on tasting the Bronze Age."

"Chicken," she teased, stepping forward to run her fingers over the contours of the ancient tool. The AI whispered facts about the artifact's use and origin, but Abigail was more captivated by the experience of feeling history under her fingertips.

"Hey, I'm all for immersive experiences, but I draw the line at licking millennia-old axes," he bantered back, the humor evident in his tone.

"Your loss," Abigail retorted.

This axe was not an actual ancient axe but a replica, like most items in the museum. The authentic artifact was stored in an offsite building, occasionally referenced when creating replacement facsimiles. Daily touch interaction would put the relic at risk. However, the replication felt authentic, or what Abigail assumed authentic would feel like. She could feel the fibers of the wood handle, rough or worn, depending on where a hand often rested. With a colder temperature than the wood handle, the stone blade had an irregular surface from chipping away. The dull edge, although thinner, was thankfully still not as thin as the axe's head. The museum had permanently affixed the axe to the display. Even this reproduction would do damage if it swung.

As Abigail moved from the axe to a series of arrowheads, Malik moved next to her to trace the axe she had just explored. He made no contact despite the proximity, but mere millimeters separated their two forms. Flirtatious but respectful, she sized up the man standing next to her. Despite them only knowing each other for just over an hour, Abigail felt wrapped up in his casual manner. She wouldn't mind if their hips were to brush. She thought to herself. I think I would like it.

They moved along the exhibit, exploring and learning, staying within touching distance but not connected. A rhythmic drumming and the hum of machinery were audible in the distance.

"Can you hear that?" she asked, curious as she reached out, her fingertips brushing against Malik's arm to help direct him to the sound.

"I think even in a museum that records the history of time,

there is still ongoing construction. Maybe the next exhibit." There was no mistaking the intimate way he responded to her touch as he replied.

"I'll need to return for the next special attraction. I hadn't realized just how much I enjoyed the museum." Abigail let her hand remain on his arm as she spoke.

"I hope to get an invitation to the next outing," Malik said, as he adjusted his arm. Abigail's hand slid down as his arm moved, and she pulled it back beside her when Malik casually took her hand in his before carrying on in the exhibit. It just felt right to Abigail. Abigail knew if she were to pull at her hand, his would slide away. He touched her without having to dominate her.

They moved together, their steps synchronized, drawn by the allure of a reproduction of a proto-human head perched on a pedestal. Abigail's hand found the sculpture before her, tracing the prominent brow ridge, the sweep of what would have been a coarse mat of hair.

"Feel this," she beckoned, guiding Malik's hand to join hers on the warm, craggy surface. Their fingers interlaced, exploring the contours as if they could divine secrets from the ridges and valleys sculpted by an unknown artist.

"Remarkable," Malik breathed out, the sound of his voice deepening, taking on a note of wonder. "I would have expected a smooth surface, but it feels porous and complicated."

"Imagine the world it saw," Abigail mused aloud, her thumb caressing the archaic cheekbone as if to coax stories from the head itself. "A world unmarred by our modern chaos."

"Or perhaps just a different kind of chaos," Malik countered, his fingers inadvertently grazing hers as they examined the hollows where eyes would have been. The contact sent a current between them, subtle yet undeniable.

"True," Abigail conceded, leaning closer to the sculpture, her body heat mingling with Malik's in the cool museum air. Her mind painted vivid strokes of prehistoric life—the hunt, the fire, the communal bonds. "But at least their chaos was straightforward. Hunt or be hunted. No pretenses."

"Quite the rugged features, wouldn't you say?" Malik's voice reverberated close to her ear, his warm breath fanning her cheek.

"Rugged, yes," Abigail agreed with a smile, "but there's a simplicity to it—a compelling rawness."

"Would you like to see how it compares to a modern-day version?" Malik teased, his tone playful. He leaned forward, inviting her exploration.

"Is this some sort of forensic test?" Reaching out, her fingertips grazed his jawline, a smooth contrast to the coarse replica. His skin was warm, alive, with a pulse that thrummed beneath her touch.

"Purely for scientific inquiry," he assured her, a chuckle coloring his words.

"Of course," Abigail said with a smirk. As her hands mapped the terrain of his forehead, a sense of wonder unfurled within her.

"Feel free to gather all the evidence you need," Malik offered, his tone light but edged with something more profound.

Her touch lingered at his brow, tracing the arch with careful curiosity. "I might take you up on that," she responded, her voice barely above a whisper.

"Then, in fairness, I should conduct my research," Malik said, his fingers poised close to her cheek but not touching. Anticipation fluttered in Abigail's chest at the prospect of an intimate connection. A connection that hung in the air, waiting for her approval. Malik's patience was endearing.

"By all means." Rotating her head so her cheek contacted the tips of his fingers. Malik's hand touched her face with a sensation that gave her goosebumps. A finger moved up her jaw, then retraced its steps to her chin. Abigail felt a twinge of excitement as his fingertips sketched the bow of her lips. She parted them, an involuntary response to the electric sensation that enveloped her. Malik repeated the motion, now with more skin to connect with.

His touch trailed lower, over the column of her neck, to the exposed skin of her collarbone. The boatneck blouse now seemed like a stroke of genius, offering just enough canvas for his perusal. Had she chosen differently, perhaps plunging, would his hands have dared to wander further? Not a horrible prospect.

"Your skin is as soft as silk," Malik murmured, almost to himself, as he traced the line of her shoulders.

"Poetic detective," she noted with amusement, her heart

hammering a rhythm against her ribs.

"More like entranced," his thumb grazing her clavicle like precious porcelain. "There's something about you... it's magnetic."

"Must be the pheromones," she joked, though her mind raced with the sheer intimacy of the moment.

"Or maybe it's just chemistry,' he countered, his voice a low timbre that matched the intensity of their connection.

"Chemistry," she echoed, wondering how something as simple as touch could speak volumes more than words.

The spell broke as a group of children invaded the space. Their sounds of joy reverberated in the museum hall. Abigail was unsure how much time had already passed in exploring their facial features or how much longer they could have remained lost in the enchantment. Much to her chagrin, they both lowered their hands. Malik again took her hand in his.

As they wandered, Malik took the opportunity to trace the details of her hand. His fingers traced her own; one finger drew out the intricate swirls on her palm that felt intoxicating. His thumb caressed her wrist. He must have been aware that her pulse had quickened. How does a light touch evoke such a powerful response? It's not like Abigail was a love-sick schoolgirl.

They strolled through the museum's next exhibit, a permanent display, a sensory garden of ancient flora. The room temperature was humid, creating an environment similar to a pre-historic jungle. The mist in the air reminded Abigail of

Club Ke Kino as she moved across the dancefloor. Unaware, she ran her teeth over her lip as she thought about it. At least she didn't have to explain why there was a sudden rush of color to her cheeks.

Malik playfully warned Abigail as she reached for a plant display. "Be careful. That's the great-great-grand botanical ancestor of a Venus flytrap. It might see you as a tasty treat."

Abigail laughed, her hand freezing in mid-air as she contemplated the risk. "I'm willing to take the risk if you are. On the count of three?" Abigail challenged.

"Let's live dangerously," he agreed, his finger intertwining with hers among the leaves. "One, two, three!"

Together, they brushed the plant's surface, which snapped back in response, causing them both to jump back and erupt into laughter.

"I guess we're just too sweet to resist," Abigail joked, a smile clear in her voice.

"Or maybe it just has impeccable taste," Malik replied, his tone light but suggestive enough to send shivers down her spine.

"Impeccable taste," she repeated, relishing the words and the idea behind them. His touch had been gentle yet daring, leaving an echoing sensation on her skin that only made her crave more.

The two of them continued to explore the exhibit. They had to push aside large palm-like leaves, sometimes at face level. The sounds of jungle life surrounded them, creating an immersive experience and shutting out the outside world.

The earthy aroma of mosses and lichens was so strong it felt almost palatable. In that moment, Abigail felt like the only two people in the entire museum or world. She wondered if she pulled him into the bushes, would he kiss her or ask what was wrong? Unsure, she decided not to take risks and held back for now.

Pushing through a set of double doors, Abigail felt the sudden blast of the air conditioner returning them to the museum's temperature-controlled area. The air was more accessible, and Abigail paused to reset her senses, taking a deep breath.

"Everything okay?" Malik asked, aware she had stopped moving and seemed to sigh.

"Everything is perfect," a dreamlike tone fluttered from another sigh.

"Perfect? I think there is still a lot more to explore. Perhaps we will exceed perfection." Malik said before taking her hand to move on to the next exhibit.

The braille sign at the next entryway advised this exhibit leveraged music and sound across history. It warned that some resonances can elicit physical sensations, and caution should be exerted: anyone with heart or pulmonary issues should bypass the exhibit through the corridor on the right.

"Sounds intriguing," Abigail said with slight trepidation.

Malik concurred, "I am happy I don't have a heart condition; I may have had to risk it."

As they crossed the threshold, there was a throbbing sensation from the floor, a deep sound that vibrated up their bodies and into their ears. "Can we hear it, or are we just feeling it?" Malik asked, his head lowering to determine if the sound got louder and closer to the floor.

Abigail stepped back across the threshold, and the sensation stopped. "I can't hear anything from here; as soon as my feet moved back, it stopped."

"So, it is sound waves without the sound? How fascinating." Malik stepped back to Abigail's side.

They both took a few steps forward to return to the exhibit. "Feels like the beat of a heart," Malik remarked, his free hand accidentally brushing against hers, sending a syncopated rhythm through her veins.

"But not our hearts. It feels older and primitive. With lots of beats rhythmically beating in unison." Abigail felt the urge to sit on the ground and feel the beats pulse up her arms. She resisted the urge, a little weary of heart disruptions that close. "If this is only the first few steps, I am eager to see what the rest of the exhibit is like."

Malik agreed, and they continued to make their way. As they passed through time, nothing compared to the initial experience. The Industrial Revolution came close with a frenzied beat of perpetual change. As they continued, the exhibits became more abstract and avant-garde. A piece entitled 'Sensation' invited visitors to feel vibrations corresponding to different emotions. Abigail pressed her hand against the panel marked 'Joy'. A laugh bubbled up from her throat as the sensation of effervescent bubbles tickled her palm and traveled up her arm to her nose. Malik did the same, and their laughter mingled in the air.

Malik pressed his hand against the next panel, his hand snapping back as he recoiled in audible pain. "What happened?" Abigail asked, placing a hand on his shoulder. Malik didn't answer. Instead, he ran his fingers over a braille sign next to the panel. With a deep breath, he placed his hand flat against the panel, his body tensing. He swallowed hard, mustering the courage to place his other hand on the panel to the right. As if by some unseen force, the tension left him, and he had an air of wonderment in his posture.

"Incredible." Malik lowered his hands from the panel. "Abigail, we just met, but these panels would be much better if you didn't know what was happening. It is asking a lot, but could I guide you?"

"Did it hurt?" Abigail's gut had already started squirming with the thought of pain.

"No, not physically, at least. It was just distressing at first. But it was worth it," Malik reassured her.

Abigail hesitated. She had promised herself to take chances, and they were in a museum; how bad could it be? After a moment of contemplation, Abigail extended her hand towards Malik.

"You will be safe." Malik directed Abigail so that she could face the panels. He took her left hand and raised it to the panel, then placed his hand behind hers. He repeated the same process with her right hand.

Malik pushed her left hand against the first panel.

A wave of fear crashed over Abigail, threatening to pull

her under. She wanted to retreat, to pull away from the unknown sensation coursing through her body. But Malik held her hands in place, grounding her. The feeling passed as Malik pushed her right hand into the second panel, leaving a strange, familiar sense behind.

"I know this feeling, but I can't name it," Abigail gasped, keeping both hands on the panels as she processed the intense experience. Abigail recalled the feeling in her apartment when fear and anger gave way to determination. "What is this?"

"Fear and self-assurance, when combined, create courage," Malik explained. "And that is what you are feeling now."

Abigail repeated the word 'courage'. It described the emotions driving her these past few days.

"This mixture of fear and confidence is not new to policing," Malik continued, taking her hands off the control panels. "I had never labeled it 'courage', but it is accurate. I apologize if it startled you." Malik added with a tinge of chagrin.

Abigail struggled to find the words to convey her emotions to Malik. How do you articulate a stranger's impact on your life, helping you discover the driving force behind your decisions? Defining and understanding the concept of 'courage' only motivated her even more.

"No need to apologize. It was an eye-opening experience. Thank you." Abigail tried to lighten the mood with a joke. "Is a panel always necessary for a man to share his feelings?"

"It depends on the man, I suppose," Malik replied in a melodic voice. "Some of us need more... physical encouragement." He had regained his flirtatious demeanor.

"Encouragement," she repeated, getting lost in their playful banter.

"Shall we try something else, then?" Malik asked, moving to stand next to her. His absence behind her made her realize just how close they had been.

"Let's keep going!" Abigail's enthusiasm rivaled a ten-year-old's.

Their path led to a sculpture that played with texture and shape; it was smooth and undulating, designed to be explored by hands alone. As Abigail traced its contours, Malik's hand found hers again, guiding her over the assorted surfaces, their fingers interlacing.

"Seems we're getting quite good at this hands-on approach," she observed, her heart rate increasing with each casual touch.

"Practice makes perfect," he replied, his breath warm against her ear. "Though I must admit, this feels like an advanced course."

"Are we passing?" she asked, a smile tugging at the corners of her mouth.

"With flying colors," he assured her, his thumb caressing the back of her hand in small, deliberate circles.

"Good," Abigail breathed out, content knowing their sensory journey was far from over. Her imagination whirred with possibility, each taste and touch a prelude to the future.

They designed the final exhibit around the obsolete items after the world lost sight of them. It was a bit underwhelming, not because she was disappointed in the lack of these items; it seemed pointless to experience something that couldn't truly be experienced anymore. But that didn't mean she couldn't have some fun and tap into her newfound 'courage.'

One display featured a decorative lamp post that stood only eight feet. Abigail led Malik over to it, wrapping her hand around its circumference. As he instinctively reached for her hand, she began running it up and down the length of the post.

"It's a remarkable artifact, isn't it?" Malik's voice cracked as if his tongue were struggling to function.

"Definitely," Abigail replied, bringing her other hand to join her fingers sliding across the surface of the post and brushing against the back of Malik's hand. "It's an impressive piece of technology," she added, trying for a seductive tone to her voice.

He chuckled in response, filling the open space with sound before pressing his hand against hers, which caused her palm to flatten hard against the metal surface.

The palpable tension coiling between them was intoxicating, their breaths mingling in harmony as each moment amplified their pulsating need. And then, she felt Malik's hot breath against her ear, stirring a fierce hunger within Abigail that begged for satiation. Abigail imagined Malik pushing her hand up higher on the post, tracing a seductive path up her arms, across her chest to caress her breasts while she remained pinned against the metal structure. The latest version of Abigail, emerging just a few nights ago, craved more. She was torn between modesty and desire. She wanted to pull off her clothes and submit as an offering if it meant his hands on her bare skin.

"Closing time, folks!" A guard's voice echoed across the hall, snapping them back to the reality of the emptying museum. The rising tension and heat fizzled out like a bucket of icy water.

Malik sighed, releasing her hand with reluctance. "Looks like our tour ends here. If I weren't working nights, I'd be curious to see where this evening might lead us."

"Such is life," Abigail agreed. Though she yearned to continue their tactile odyssey beyond the museum walls, she didn't want to appear needy. "Duty calls, right?"

"Always," he said with a rueful smile. "Do you want to try a first-not-blind date?"

"How about a second date? It is easier on the brain." Abigail wanted to say something flirty like, "Why reset the counter?" but didn't think she could deliver it without tripping over her words. Hours from now, she'd think of a sexy retort. The poor man will miss the sexy talk. Abigail will have to handle his side for him.

As they made their way out into the evening air, Abigail let herself savor the thought of their subsequent encounter—a chance to peel back another layer of the intriguing man who had turned a simple museum visit into an unexpected journey of the senses.

Abigail lay in the comfort of her bed, the gentle hum of the city's night song flitting through her open window. The crisp smell of citrus zest lingered in her memory, a phantom presence that teased her senses with the faintest whisper. "Would you have dared?" she murmured into the darkness, her voice barely louder than a breath as she imagined Malik lying beside her, his detective's acumen turned towards mapping the secrets of her body.

Her fingers tentatively began their investigation, tracing the soft expanse of her abdomen just as they had explored the cool marble at the museum.

"But would I have had the courage to reciprocate?" Abigail pondered aloud, allowing her hands to graduate to the gentle slopes of her hips. The thought of his touch replacing hers sent a thrill racing down her spine. She could almost feel his fingertips skating across her skin, pausing at each delicate rise and dip as if committing her contours to memory.

Abigail moved a hand to her collarbone; her fingers lingered where Malik's touch had ignited a subtle fire. He was confident, yet gentle, when he touched her. At no point had he tried to overpower her. She heard his voice in her head, "For scientific purposes only, Abigail," as she traced her fingers between her breasts. His hands would have been purposeful and methodical as he moved his fingers over the contours and peaks of her breasts.

Abigail let her fingers glide across her taunt nipples. She

felt a small wave of pleasure, followed by disappointment. As much as she left empowered to explore her own body, she realized she would not be satisfied until she had the real thing. It's Detective Malik Callahan, no doubt.

Chapter 14

The echoes of distant laughter reverberated through the corridor of the Sensma, a cinematic marvel that rose from the ashes of the Sightless Plague. Abigail's hand trailed along the textured wall, a guide to the entertainment sensation of space around her. The air was infused with the scent of buttered popcorn—a nostalgic tribute to the theaters of the past.

"Malik, do you think they have lights in here? For the AI cameras, I mean," Abigail mused, her head tilting so that her ear could better hear the noise from the ceiling. It had an electric buzz sound, which she thought could be lighting.

"Probably, night vision technology has limits, so lights in a place like this would assist technology. Even the robotic ushers could use the help to avoid spilling our drinks. Many places that once were low-light areas, movie theaters, bars, and clubs are well-lit now to help AI with everyone's safety."

Nothing like having a police detective to educate you on personal safety. Abigail found it reassuring.

It had been a week since Abigail and Malik had explored the Museum. Neither of their schedules had aligned for a proper outing. They had exchanged flirty messages and managed a quick 'coffee date' one afternoon. Coffee had been pleasant but rushed. Abigail needed to return to school before the next period, and Malik was exhausted from finishing his work. The tension was electric between them.

Abigail and Malik, guided by a symphony of subtle cues from their AI companions, navigated the textured floor until they reached their designated double pod. The pod had an accompanying wardrobe and a safe to store their belongings. Removing clothing was completely optional, but the pod provided tactile-like experiences that were more effective in direct skin contact.

Abigail hung up her spring jacket and began unbuttoning her blouse to disrobe.

"Let me know when you are done, and I will get ready." Abigail heard Malik's voice, which sounded uncomfortable, as if he was speaking in the opposite direction. Abigail regretted not confirming Malik's comfort level before disrobing. She should not have made assumptions.

"Malik, did you turn away? Is this making you uneasy?" Abigail inquired, pausing before hanging up her blouse. If he felt uncomfortable, she would put it back on. "We don't need to undress if you don't want the tactile experience."

"I, uh, just don't want to make you feel uneasy," Malik

replied, still speaking in the other direction.

"How very polite of you. However, it is just like wearing a bathing suit. It's not like we are getting naked. Should I continue?"

"Yes, for sure. It is the best way to enjoy the experience."

Abigail removed the remaining excess clothing. "I am done now. Entering the left side of the pod, you can safely prepare," she responded, making a note to keep her tone neutral. She did not want to make Malik more ill at ease by judging his comfort level.

Abigail slid into the double occupancy pod. The chair fit the contours of her shape, and she waited in a partially reclined position for Malik to join her. It felt waxy under her bare skin, and the smell of disinfectant from the last cleaning lingered.

Malik's weight, taking his spot, jostled the pod slightly. Abigail's confidence slipped now, realizing that Malik sat next to her in likely just his briefs. Would it be too forward to ask how much he had disrobed? Perhaps she should have considered how much skin would be involved in their third date when she suggested the cinema. Instead of details, she asked, "You good?"

"Yup." Malik provided a curt reply. Was that an indication of unease?

Abigail began discussing the movie to distract them both from their state of undress. "Modern-day Tarzan, huh? I'm curious how Jane will handle the jungle this time around." Abigail aimed for a playful tone, echoing the comedic undertones expected in the performance.

"Ah, but remember, it's not Jane—it's Joanna, the indomitable jungle queen," Malik corrected her with mock gravity. "And our scientist, well, I hear he can't even tie his shoelaces without a manual." Abigail could sense that his voice was directed at her instead of straight out or to the other side, hopeful that it was a sign whatever had bothered him before had been resolved.

"Sounds like my kind of man," Abigail jested. She imagined the helpless male protagonist floundering through vines and foliage, a thought that tickled a chuckle from her throat.

A light series of audible beats indicated there were only two minutes until the show would start. Abigail pulled at the strap that raised the technological 'blanket' up over their legs and torso. The blanket served as a haptic sensory interface that would send signals to their skin, placing them in the show. The blanket was heavy, most likely to generate the most skin-to-technology ratio. She thought someone who was claustrophobic would struggle with the blanket and enclosure as the pod hood closed over them. "You aren't claustrophobic, are you?" asked too late if he was.

"No, not at all." Malik sounded amused. "Are you?"

"Gosh, no. I like small spaces. There is something comforting about being able to touch the limits of your mobility. However, that assumes I am not trapped in a small space. That would freak me out." Abigail shared. "But it would probably freak nearly the entire population of the planet."

"I am just happy the top of the pod is not low. I would not feel good if I couldn't sit upright without smashing my head or face into the top." Malik added.

A final beep indicated the film was going to begin.

The surrounding space began filling with the lush sounds of an imaginary jungle. Speakers hidden throughout the pod recorded sounds of birds and animals. At the same time, a scent diffuser emitted the earthy aroma of soil and sweet notes of tropical fruits. The temperature in their theater shifted subtly, the humidity rising to complete the immersive sensation of being deep within a verdant rainforest.

"Joanna's domain seems to have quite the ambiance," Malik murmured, and Abigail could feel the vibrations of his words through the armrest they shared. When Abigail's arm touched Malik's, she could confirm that he had removed his shirt, at least. His skin was warm against hers, and she could feel each hair tickling at her skin.

"Indeed. The environment is lush. It reminds me of the flora exhibit. I wonder if there will be carnivorous plants set on eating our blundering scientist." Abigail was pleased she could relate today to the date a week prior. Would it help Malik remember both the conflicting ease and tension between them? She wanted to feel both again.

"Given it's a comedy, anything is possible. Perhaps a singing pitcher plant reminiscent of Little Shop of Horrors," came Malik's response, a ripple of laughter in his voice. His thumb swept over her knuckles in a lazy caress that felt carefree.

"If there is, Joanna is sure to have to rescue the scientist from the plant's clutches." Abigail felt a kinship growing with Joanna. Her confidence was growing. Her mind was adrift in the experience's novelty, yet anchored by the touch that tethered her to the moment.

The movie begins with Felix, the fish-out-of-water scientist, panting, tripping, and stumbling, trying to navigate the jungle floor. With each slip, the pod would jerk slightly, pushing or pulling Abigail and Malik closer or apart. "Maybe I should have put the seatbelt on," Abigail said after suddenly jerking to one side. "With all the technological advancements, the cross-chest seatbelt is still uncomfortable for bustier women." Her body flushed with heat as she realized that she just called attention to both her breasts and their size. Would he want to check it out for himself, she wondered and hoped.

"Yes, it is a little bouncing in here," Malik replied, not mentioning her seatbelt problem. "I'm not trying to put any lecherous moves on you. We could put the armrest up, and I can hold you closer so we don't keep knocking into each other," Malik suggested, not lecherous but a little flirtatious.

"It is probably the best course of action for our safety." Abigail kept her response light and detached, but could not help the playful tone in her voice.

"Yes, just for safety," Malik repeated, echoing the 'just for scientific inquiry' from the week before. Those words had led to physical exploration; would these words elicit the same response? Abigail reminded herself to focus on the movie, not trying to orchestrate a steamy romance of their own. Malik raised the armrest and reached his arm overhead towards Abigail. As if rehearsed, she raised her head and torso, letting Malik slide his arm easily behind the small of her back. She settled back down, and Malik shifted them closer.

They now touched from Abigail's shoulder to thigh. With the next bounce, they remained fixed together, with just a tiny amount of friction between them. As Felix fell to the jungle floor, succumbing to the heat and exhaustion, Abigail and Malik remained laced together.

The following scene describes Joanna crouched over the unconscious man. Joanna poked and sniffed as she moved about Felix's prolonged form, researching the strange beast. The heady aroma of wild orchids wafted around Abigail as the auditory landscape changed, birdsong and the distant cry of an exotic creature filling the air. She could almost feel the dappled sunlight she knew must be filtering through a canopy that existed only in their shared imagination. Beside her, Malik shifted in his seat, reminding her just how close they were.

Joanna raised the man's hand and released it, letting it flop again. Joanna was not gentle as she straddled the man's waist, leaning forward to inspect his facial features. She traced his brow and down along his nose, inserting a finger into each nostril. Malik restrained a laugh; Abigail could feel the slight bounce in his chest. "I am thankful you were not so thorough in your exploration." Malik's words tickled her ears, increasing the humor of the situation. How did so many details about this film remind them of their first encounter?

As Abigail was about to respond, she heard the narrator describe Joanna grabbing Felix by the chin to force his mouth open as she stuck her other hand in to trace his teeth. Unable to speak, Abigail just laughed at the absurdity of it all. Malik, unable to hold it back, joined Abigail's laughter. They both regained control as Felix awakened and sat up, getting his first glimpse of the jungle queen.

As the narrative in the jungle unfolded, Abigail and Malik fell into a comfortable silence, engrossed in the film. Their state of undress became familiar, and no longer distracted Abigail from the movie's ambiance. She was lost in the jungle, along with Felix, who had wandered off from Joanna's safe presence.

"Sounds like Dr. Hapless is about to encounter his first vine." Malik's voice cut through the film's enchantment. The audio snapped, the sound of twigs breaking under Felix's feet. Abigail could picture the clumsy scientist swinging wildly, a mental image that made her giggle.

The jungle sounds swirled around Abigail and Malik, and the sensory theater's state-of-the-art acoustics simulated a cacophony of chirping insects and rustling leaves. The earthy scent of wet soil and wildflowers was pumped through the air vents.

"Is it getting hot in here?" Malik asked, pushing the blanket down his torso. So much skin was beside her, resulting in chills down her spine. The pod was warm, partially because of the atmospheric settings and their shared body heat.

Abigail laughed, the sound fluttering out nervously as she adjusted herself in the seat that seemed to have shrunk since they first sat down. "I think it's the latter. We must be nearing the heart of the rainforest."

Their thighs brushed beneath the privacy of the shared blanket draping over their laps, an innocent contact that raced Abigail's pulse.

"Malik..." Abigail breathed out his name, a confession acknowledging the craving that had been kindled within her.

"Your skin is so soft," he murmured, his fingertips brushing against the nape of her neck and weaving through the strands of her hair with gentle reverence. "I am hypnotized by how it feels, how you feel, like everything I've ever wanted is right here in my arms."

She tilted her head into his caress, savoring the intimacy. "Thank you," she whispered back, not trusting her voice to carry more than those two words loaded with unspoken questions and burgeoning desires.

"Thank me by letting me hold you closer," he said, pulling her into the curve of his arm. Her head rested against his shoulder, fitting perfectly into place as if molded from the very essence of compatibility.

Malik kept up the loving caress, his hand weaving through the silky strands of her hair, drifting down her arm in a teasing promise before returning upwards. His touch was tantalizingly slow and sensual, like a favorite song played on repeat.

Abigail responded in kind. Her agile fingers danced across

the rugged terrain of his chest, playing out an intimate melody of their own. Absorbed in her world, she forgot about the budding romance between Felix and Joanna, letting the heat between her and Malik eclipse everything else.

Malik, too, had abandoned the pretense of experiencing the movie. His focus was solely on Abigail now—on each enticing curve of her body that beckoned his hands and begged for exploration. His hand grazed against the lace of her bra tentatively before applying more pressure with each passing moment. Malik's thumb outlined her nipple through the lace fabric, stirring it into a stiff peak before languidly returning to caress her waist. Abigail moaned in frustration at the sudden lack of contact, an unattended breast pulsing with unfulfilled desire.

She could play this game too, Abigail thought devilishly. Taking advantage of her proximity to his muscular chest, she pressed feather-light kisses there, letting her teeth graze his skin. Reaching his nipple, she gave it an unexpected flicker of her warm tongue before laying back down teasingly against his solid frame and resting a steady hand on his chiseled abdomen to keep him on edge.

A moment passed, perhaps only three seconds, and Abigail could not wait for Malik's next move. Seizing control, she spun forward in one fluid movement, now straddling his sculpted torso. He instinctively gripped her ass tight, pulling her close.

Malik did not resist; he took the new position as an opportunity to reciprocate, exploring her chest now. He kissed, sucked, and nipped at her flushed flesh through the thin lace barrier with fervor—this time alternating between both peaks, ensuring each received equal attention. It was blissful torment.

Abigail unclipped her bra from behind, pulling it down and away. She pressed her chest into Malik's attentive mouth, wanting more. Malik obliged until his mouth retreated. Hot air moved across Abigail's now wet breasts. His breath panted mere inches from her body.

"Not like this," he said.

"Not like this?" Abigail questioned, her voice barely above a whisper.

"Not yet," Malik answered firmly. "I want to, my god, I want to. But I want more first."

"Okay, what more would you like?" Abigail tried her best to sound seductive and coy.

"Not like that. His hands reached the small of her back. He lightly kissed her jawline and continued, "I want to look back at our beginning and remember a long sensual exploration, not something fast and messy because a movie will end in a few minutes." Malik kissed the tip of her nose.

Abigail found it challenging to process the words he spoke. Still charged, her brain felt woozy as she took it all in. Sensual exploration sounds good; they could continue that. Then the rest of Malik's words set in. Oh my god, the movie will end any minute, and they would have been caught for sure. Still cradled in Malik's arms, Abigail shifted back to her seat, breathless, embarrassed, and frustrated. It wasn't a flat-out rejection, but Malik was quick to put the brakes on while she was lost in the sensation. As a police officer, he may have been more aware of his behavior and the inappropriateness of their conduct in the pod; at least, that was what Abigail assumed.

They lay there silently for a few minutes, unsure how to proceed. "Abigail," Malik broke the silence. "I don't want this to come out wrong. But, I don't do relationships, casual or committed. It was just never something I saw for myself. Since meeting you, I feel like my world has been turned upside down, and I can't imagine it going back." Malik took a deep breath before continuing in a rush, "I want a relationship with you. I want to make sure that is what you want as well."

His declaration moved Abigail. It did little to cool the fire in her belly, but she respected his honesty. "Sounds wonderful." She wasn't sure exactly what she should have said next. Should she thank him? Provide verbal consent? Consent to what? Clarify what 'relationship' means to him? Instead of adding anything else, she returned to listening to the movie.

Despite Abigail's confusion, returning to casual was simple. She found everything about being around Malik easy. Abigail grabbed the container of contraband she had stashed between the seats. The glass container still felt the warmth from the baking. She opened the box and offered the cookies to Malik.

"These are delicious," Malik said, savoring the flavors on his tongue. "What are they?"

"Lemon and rosemary melts. It's a cookie sort of like a shortbread but far easier to make." Abigail took one for herself, popping the confection into her mouth. The moment it hit her tongue, the sweet herbaceous flavors electrified her taste buds like drops of sunshine. "I love cooking and baking. I was thinking of starting a blog." A timid blush grew on her cheeks. Despite sharing an intimate moment, sharing an unrealized dream felt more revealing.

"Stop thinking and start doing!" Malik urged, reaching out for another cookie. "May I have another?"

"Yes, you may." Abigail beamed with unseen pride. Despite having Tessa and Imani's support, Malik's endorsement felt inspiring. Abigail settled into the movie's last few minutes with a warm sense of pride down her spine, enclosed in a pod that smelled of lemon, rosemary, and the jungle. In that moment, nothing better could be imagined.

Once the movie finished, they shifted out of their seats, stretching back to full height. Malik suggested she get dressed first. "Malik, you know 85% of my body right now; I don't think we need to be so modest." Abigail was feeling around the pod for her missing bra. She could not keep leaving her bras behind.

"I find you distracting. I'd probably put my shirt on my legs and tie my pants around my chest." Malik comically explained.

"Don't be silly. Just come get dressed so we can get out of here." Abigail instructed.

Chapter 15

A gentle breeze played with Abigail's hair as they left the cinema. The evening breeze helped cool the excitement of a few nerve endings, still holding out for more sensual pleasures. "I guess there is no point inviting you back to my place for a drink? Hint-hint, nudge-nudge," Abigail joked.

Malik let out a deep laugh, releasing all the tension in his body. "As tempting as that invitation is, I think it best if I don't, for tonight, at least. But if it is okay with you, I'd like to walk you home," Malik asked.

"Yes, I'd like that," Abigail agreed, lacing her arm around his and turning toward her apartment complex. "So, Detective Callahan, tell me something about yourself."

"Is this an interrogation, Ms. Sorensen?" Malik inquired.

Abigail mustered up her best imitation of a crime drama. "Not officially, but it may help your cause if we can come to some sort of understanding."

"Well, then, I am happy to oblige. I had a typical upbringing: two loving parents, a younger sister, and many dogs over the years. Very normal."

"Aren't you a wealth of knowledge? I feel like I know you so much better now. I'll share that I have one mouth like most of the population." sarcasm dripping from Abigail's tone.

"Touché, let me see...My family is about an hour from here, in the country. I moved to the city to join the police department." Malik only mildly elaborated, nothing she didn't already know.

Probing Malik along, Abigail asked, "Why did you want to go into law enforcement?"

"You could say it was a calling. My skill sets that made solving puzzles come easily to me. I wanted to be a detective, which meant the police force. Perhaps I could have been a private investigator. I had never considered it."

"What was the first case you broke?" Abigail continued the polite interrogation.

"Oh, that was the hardest one of my career. 'Who was stealing the eggs from Farmer Charlie's coop?' had me up for several nights when I was four."

Abigail sputtered a laugh, "Four? It seems early to be chasing down clues. So, who was the culprit?"

"Farmer Charlie's son Charlie Junior. The poor boy wanted a break from scrambled eggs every morning."

"How did you catch the egg bandit?" Abigail jokingly

pressed.

"I saw him sneak into the coop from a perch in my treehouse. Charlie Junior was caught and managed to turn his life around before becoming a criminal mastermind."

"You saw him?" Abigail's curiosity was piqued.

"Well, no, not really 'saw him', more my AI saw him and let me know. I directed my AI to keep a watch." Malik clarified.

Abigail thought about it momentarily, "So, would that make your AI the lead detective?'

"No." Malik's sharpness resulted in a reflexive step back. Malik adjusted his tone: "Sorry, officers are a tad sensitive regarding AIs. While vital, they lack the intuition and drive to solve a case. They observe and relay facts." Abigail realized she had hit a nerve.

"Yes, I could see that. The AI helps direct students, but I am the teacher who creates the learning plan. I want them to be successful. The AI has no vested interest in the child." Abigail attempted to relate to Malik's relationship with AI. "Do you feel the same way about your personal AI?" Despite Jules being an AI, Abigail felt connected to the synthetic voice.

"It has its conveniences, but there is no genuine connection despite the coding. I am not anti-AI per se, but with work and home, I feel a little over-directed by the constant scrutiny. Enough AI. Let's talk about humans. Tell me about yourself."

Abigail couldn't imagine her life without Jules, a dear friend she never got to see. Anti-AI groups were convinced they were watching to destroy us all, but Abigail had never been swayed by the propaganda. She had also never had to defend herself or her work.

Abigail returned to Malik's question. "You still haven't done a background check?" Initially, Abigail's stomach dropped at the prospect. However, she realized a weight would be lifted if he knew. It would no longer loom over her unsaid.

"I said I wouldn't, so no. If there is something I should know, I'd rather hear it from you than a police file. When you want to tell me," It was like Malik could read her mind.

"It's nothing illegal. Well, nothing I did that was illegal." Abigail took a few steps to distance herself. She scrunched her fists into tight balls, holding her emotions in check. Blurt it out, she said to herself. "I was attacked a few years ago, and my purse was stolen. The broken ribs healed, but my spirit is still on the mend."

As the last words left her mouth, Malik spun her around in a tight hug, stroking her back. "My god, Abigail. That is terrible. I don't know what to say." Malik gave her a tighter squeeze.

Despite her resolve, Abigail felt the hot tears well up in her eyes and trickle down her face. A small choking cry gurgled to the surface, but she suppressed any sobs from escaping. Malik continued to stroke her back in soothing circles while she regained her composure. "Ugh, I'm sorry. I didn't want you to see me like this. Weepy and weak," she said, wiping her face.

"Abi, you don't need to hide from me. What happened to you was traumatic. You should never apologize for your feelings." Malik said reassuringly. "Thank you for telling me. Now, I don't have to keep worrying you were a criminal mastermind that I would have to arrest one day." He released Abigail from his embrace and took her hand.

"Oh, yes, about my criminal enterprise..." Abigail started.

Malik pulled her into a side hug. "Plausible deniability, say no more." He kissed the top of her head.

Abigail felt lighter after sharing the experience with Malik. In a short time, he provided more support than Ryker ever had. Where her tears had made Ryker cringe and literally leave her—Malik held her close.

They continued the walk back to Abigail's apartment in pleasant conversation. Abigail shared more about growing up in the city and shenanigans with Tessa. Malik shared about his transition from country sleuth to city detective.

Abigail's stomach fluttered with imaginary butterflies when they reached the apartment. "So, I guess this is goodnight?" With hope she asked, but prepared for the likely confirmation.

With a regretful moan, Malik let go of her hand. "Yes, this is goodnight." Malik pulled her close and kissed the top of her head. "Let me know when you are at the door."

Shocked there was no deep goodbye kiss, Abigail shuffled to the door in a daze. Is that it? She thought. She had expected more tension and 'will he, won't he' possibilities. Confused, she called back when she was at the door and said one final goodnight. Disappointment sunk into every cell in her body.

Abigail's key slid into the lock with an air of betrayal, its metallic click echoing her tumultuous thoughts as she entered the dim sanctuary of her apartment. The door closed behind her with a soft thud, sealing her within the walls, that now felt too close for comfort.

"Welcome home, Abigail," chirped Jules as it reactivated inside, its voice a balm to her frayed nerves. She shrugged off her jacket and let it fall carelessly onto the floor below the hook.

"Thanks," she muttered, pressing her fingertips to her temples a moment before instinctively securing the locks.

"Would you like to talk about what is troubling you?" Jules inquired.

"Malik didn't kiss me goodnight. Well, he pecked me goodnight, but didn't kiss me like I thought he would." Abigail blurted out, pacing her living room like a caged animal seeking an escape. "Did something go wrong during our walk home?"

"I am not sure, Abigail. You dismissed me from your date. I only reactivated with your entrance to the apartment." Jules rationally explained.

"It was a rhetorical question." Abigail snapped at Jules.

"My apologies. Please let me know when I can be of service." Was Jules' guilt tripping her, she thought? Can AI be passive-aggressive?

"Is everyone going bonkers tonight, or is it just me?" Abigail felt exhausted and slumped down in an armchair.

"If that question was directed at me, I can assure you I am functioning well within parameters. Would you elaborate on the conclusion that no kiss equals bonkers?" Okay, that was Jules patronizing her, she thought.

"If you must know, the movie went very well. There was lots of kissing, and the goodbye kiss was like I was a child or his sister. I can only assume he lost interest in me sometime between the show and getting home." Abigail huffed into the armchair, reminiscent of a sulking child.

"There is an old English proverb about assuming would you like to hear it? I think it may apply to this situation." Jules offered.

"No, Jules, I don't need to hear about me being an ass. Thank you."

"Very well, Abigail. I will point out that there could be several reasons for the change in physical contact."

"Like what, oh wise one?" Abigail grunted back.

"Perhaps Detective Callahan was showing restraint because he needed to return home to use the facilities. There is anecdotal evidence that humans often prefer their homes for such activities. Or, perhaps he worried he could not control himself," the helpful AI offered.

"Oh great, it is either he needed to take a crap or would have not been able to leave. You forgot maybe he is married and had to get home to his wife and two adorable children."

"Searching...public records do not show that Detective Callahan has a wife or children. Abigail, you may be the one going bonkers this evening," Jules said.

"Maybe," Abigail pouted.

"Abigail, you have had several unpleasant encounters across the last few weeks; perhaps you are looking for problems where they do not exist?" Jules suggested.

Abigail's shoulders slumped. Was she so terrified of letting someone in that she'd latch onto any excuse to push them away?

"Abigail, self-sabotage is not conducive to forming meaningful relationships," Jules chided softly, its words a gentle reprimand.

"Since when did you become a relationship guru?" Abigail scoffed, yet the truth in Jules' observation stung. "Okay," she exhaled, mustering the courage to be vulnerable. "Let's try this again." She reached for her communicator and composed a message.

"Malik, fancy grabbing drinks tomorrow night?" Her finger hovered over the send button, a cocktail of hope and hesitation swirling within her.

The reply came almost instantly, like a comet streaking across a starless sky. "I'd love to, Abigail. Thank you."

His quick reply sent a pleasant shiver across her skin, pushing away her doubts. He was eager to see her again.

"Excellent choice, Abigail," Jules said, its tone approving.

"Thank you, oh wise one," Abigail mocked her persistent

AI. Jules' would always have her back. She thought loyalty may have been a programmable feature, but each personal AI seemed to suit a person's needs. It was hard to determine what was self-taught after years of partnership. "I mean it, Jules; thank you for everything you do."

"You are welcome, Abigail."

"Goodnight." Abigail pushed herself out of the seat and shuffled her way to another night of restless sleep. Tomorrow, I will not let him off with a peck on the head, Abigail promised herself.

Chapter 16

"Tessa, I need your help." Abigail felt frantic as she dragged her friend into her apartment the following day. She let out a loud, insuppressible yawn. Nights without good sleep were taking a toll.

"What's up, buttercup?" Tessa affectionately made light of Abigail's panic.

"Our goodnight kiss was barely a graze on my head. What if we went from can't keep our hands off each other to friend zone?" Abigail's heart pounded in her chest as sweat beaded on her skin. She had already checked for a fever in case she was ill. "I told him about the attack after our date; maybe he can't see me as sexy anymore?" The last words eked out of her mouth; terrified that was the reason for the change in demeanor the previous night.

"Abi, give yourself a shake, or I will." Tessa's voice dropped an octave, her stern tone that of an impatient parent. "That is an absolute load of bullshit. It is insulting to you and this man. I want no more of this defeatist talk."

Abigail involuntarily responded to Tessa's reprimand by sitting up straighter. Stunned, her voice failed to utter a response.

"So, no more? Good." Tessa praised Abigail's silence. "From my limited information, Malik seems like a good person. There is an excellent reason for his behavior, even if we don't understand it yet. As for you, my dear friend, you must get out of your head." Tessa lectured. "You overthink everything. I guess that is why you are exhausted this morning. A night of scenario playing in your head?"

Abigail was unsure if the question was rhetorical or if she should answer. Since her voice now worked, she replied, "Yes."

"As I thought, I want no more of this. You are strong, vibrant, and sexy as hell. Repeat it," Tessa ordered.

Abigail whispered out the words. Tessa made her repeat several times until it was delivered with confidence.

"Now, the truth bomb. Maybe things don't work out, but that is Malik's loss. If he can't see how utterly fabulous you are, he doesn't deserve all your sexiness." Tessa said.

"I don't want that. How do I get him to want me? I am out of experience; how do I move from kissing to ripping off clothes and rounds of awesome sex?" Abigail whined.

"You don't make him want you. He either does or he doesn't. That is not the question." Scolding, Tessa returned to the conversation. "When you were younger, and someone wasn't into you, or you weren't into them, what did you do?"

"Found someone else?" Abigail answered.

"Yes, you found someone else. And if you wanted to know if someone wanted sex, what did you do?"

"Asked them?" Abigail continued to question her answer.

"Hell, yes! Ask for what you want and don't pursue someone who doesn't want the same." Tessa's hands slammed down on the table in excitement. "Abi, I say this because I love you. Kick yourself in the ass, take a shower because you stink, and when you meet up with the detective, ask him to—"

Abigail cut her off. "Nope, don't finish that. I know what to ask." Preventing a detailed execution plan infused with Tessa's joie de vie.

"What? I was only going to suggest he French braid your hair," Tessa replied innocently.

"Mm-hmm, I am sure. Maybe something French. Thank you for the reality check."

"Any time, my dear. You can repay me with a box of cookies." Tessa eased into the apartment, taking a seat. "Go, make some cookies. It will calm your nerves and feed my sweet tooth. I'll lounge here on the couch and listen to a story."

Before Abigail walked away, Tessa added. "Wait, on second thought, go have a shower and then make cookies. I'll put on a pot of coffee for when you come out."

Abigail headed off to the shower, as instructed. Perhaps Tessa should become a motivational speaker because Abigail felt empowered again.

As promised, when Abigail returned to the kitchen, a carafe of coffee awaited her on the counter. She poured herself a mug and got started on a batch of cookies. Lemon and rosemary had been her staple cookie the last year. But for Tessa's special cookies, she would make something new, a flavor that would match Tessa's personality. She took ginger from the freezer and a fresh orange. Grating each into her mixture, Abigail made orange gingersnaps.

The cookies were still warm when she brought a tray to Tessa in the living room. "Give it a few more minutes to cool," she warned.

"Can't. I have been stuck on this couch, smelling the most divine scent. I cannot wait." Tessa grabbed the hot cookie and took a bite. "Wow, that is refreshing, quite the zing."

"I am happy you like them. I will box them up before you leave. Thank you for the reality check."

"No problem. I enjoy bossing people around. It is a gift." Tessa took another cookie before she continued. "Speaking of bossy people. Have you talked to your mom since the anniversary party?"

"Great segue. No, I haven't spoken to her. I thought about calling. I could say I was busy, but that is just an excuse. If I am honest with myself, and you, I want my mom to call and apologize." Abigail took an aggressive bite of her cookie, frustrated by the situation.

"I can see that. It was an unusually truthful moment between you both. She was completely out of line." Tessa offered support for her friend. "But you are the bigger person. I can't see your mom calling unless she needs something, and you don't want that call. If I were you, I would call. She might never admit she was wrong, but she will try to make it right in her own way."

"Maybe. I don't want my dad to serve as the middleman at the next family dinner. But for today, I have more important things to do."

"Hell yes, you do. I am heading out now so you can get your sexy self ready. Call me later with all the details." Tessa exited her chair and the apartment. Abigail didn't even have time to pack up the cookies.

Chapter 17

The clinking of glassware and the murmur of conversation enveloped Abigail as she entered the bar. The rich aroma of aged whiskey and the subtle undertone of fermentation immediately bombarded her senses. She moved with practiced grace, her internal positioning guiding her to the reserved spot where Malik would be waiting. The air was dense with anticipation, a palpable electric charge that seemed to gravitate towards their meeting point.

"Abigail," came Malik's voice, a touch more hesitant than she remembered, as if he were measuring each syllable before they left his lips. "You made it."

"I wouldn't miss it," Abigail responded, her tone light, trying to ease the nerves she detected in his greeting.

They settled into their seats, the leather creaking beneath them. The initial awkwardness hung between them like a delicate veil, one that Abigail was determined to lift.

They ordered drinks, and Abigail got the stout she had wanted on blind date number two. Malik opted for soda water.

"Do you not drink alcohol? Not that there is anything wrong with that."

"It's not that I don't drink. I am just selective of when and where. Part of me feels like I am always on duty when outside my home," Malik explained. "I need to keep a level head, in case..." He let the possibilities remain open. Abigail thought there could be several things that a detective might need to intervene in.

As their drinks arrived, Abigail asked, "Does it bother you if I have my drink?"

"No, not at all. Maybe one day I will hang up the detective persona for a night and relax with you."

Abigail absently moved her finger along the surface of the glass, feeling the cold condensation move along with her finger. Abigail noted he had not yet taken her hand or even touched her this evening.

Silence overtook the table as they both sipped their drinks. Eventually, Malik broke the silence. "I wanted to apologize about last night," he said, fidgeting with his glass. "I kept repeating in my head from the theater to your house to behave like a gentleman and forgot how to act like a man attracted to a woman." If a blush had a sound, Abigail was pretty sure she could hear the blush in Malik's voice. "I was so worried if I touched you, it would not have stopped there. I am sorry for acting weird."

"You do not know how happy I am to hear that." Abigail released a breath she didn't know she was holding. "I was so worried something had gone wrong on our walk home."

"Wrong, opposite of wrong. It took every ounce of willpower in me not to ask to come in." Malik finally touched her hand.

"So, was today utterly uncomfortable for you as well? I have been fretting about tonight since I messaged you."

A chuckle rumbled from Malik's chest, low and growl-like. "Something like that. It's... been an odd day. I thought about canceling or messaging you my apology so I wouldn't have to explain in person. I must have played out this conversation a hundred times today."

"Oh my gosh, me too." Abigail leaned forward, intertwining their fingers. The contact sent a warmth spiraling up her arm.

Their shared foolishness provided a bond that brought their conversation back to the normal easiness they had known. The conversation remained light and on neutral topics. Abigail told Malik about Venus and her demanding palette. Malik also had a pet, a dog named Baxter.

"Is Baxter a service dog for the police or a personal service dog?" Abigail asked. No one she knew had a cat that provided a service outside the home, but cats were trained to help. Dogs were commonplace to assist their human.

"Neither. Maybe one day. He has too much energy and failed trials for both functions. He is so sweet that I only took him home as a pet."

Their banter flowed more freely, punctuated by laughter and the occasional clink of glasses as they toasted to trivial confessions and shared secrets. The surrounding space receded, becoming a blur as their world shrank to the bubble of their existence.

"Careful, or we'll give the AIs something to gossip about," Abigail teased, feeling his hand rest on her knee, a touch that suggested promises yet to be fulfilled.

"Let them talk," Malik said, the earlier restraint replaced with a bubbling confidence.

"Exactly," Abigail agreed, her heart racing, the uncertainty of the day dissolving under the weight of their undeniable connection.

The air was thick with the scent of spiced liquor and the hum of bass notes from the bar's sound system, a tactile symphony that vibrated through their bodies. Abigail felt Malik's breath against her neck, warm and steady, as his lips found the tender skin beneath her earlobe, sending a shiver down her spine.

"Abigail," he murmured, his voice a silken thread weaving through her senses. "Come home with me."

His plea was a soft vibration against her flesh, a question laden with desire and something more—a longing for connection that resonated deep within her own heart. She nestled closer to him, her hands exploring the contours of his back, feeling the play of muscles beneath his shirt.

"I want to," Abigail confessed, her words infused with a yearning that mirrored his own. The taste of his kiss lingered on her lips, a tantalizing blend of sweetness and heat that promised more.

"Then let's go," Malik said, his fingers interlacing with hers in a tender and insistent grip. His touch was a language she had understood intimately, each movement a word, each caress a sentence that told her of his affection and need.

Together, they stood, their movements synchronized like a dance perfected over time. The crowd's thrum receded into the background, replaced by the rhythm of their quickening pulses as they moved toward the exit in unison.

As they burst out of the restaurant and into the fantastic night, the crisp air filled their lungs, sobering yet invigorating. They paused momentarily, chests heaving, the electric charge of anticipation crackling between them. Without saying more, Malik led the way.

Chapter 18

Abigail's fingers interlaced with Malik's as they ascended the last steps to his duplex, her heart a staccato rhythm against her ribs. The cool evening breeze played with strands of her hair, carrying the faintest scent of jasmine from some unseen nocturnal garden.

"Here we are," Malik announced, a hint of breathlessness in his voice that didn't entirely stem from the climb. He fumbled at the door, digits dancing clumsily over the electronic lock with an inelegance that belied his usual dexterity.

"Need a hand?" Abigail teased, her head cocked to one side.

"Got it!" he declared triumphantly, though not before the AI's calm voice intervened. "Door unlocked." They stepped into the warmth of his home.

"Make yourself at home," Malik said, touching her elbow and steering her towards the living space.

The air rippled with anticipation, like the charged silence before a storm. Abigail perched on the edge of a plush sofa. The fabric was soft beneath her fingertips. She heard the creak of Malik's movements as he crossed the room and the clink of glassware from presumably the kitchen.

"Thought you'd come back wielding something a bit stronger," she teased when Malik returned, presenting her with chamomile tea.

"You mentioned you enjoyed teas. I picked up a box," he replied, easing himself into the armchair next to her, the sound of the fabric against the fabric as he settled in.

"You do know chamomile tea is for helping people fall asleep."

Malik took the cup of tea from Abigail's hand and returned to the kitchen, where he brought them a glass of child cola. "Well, that says something different from chamomile tea," Abigail complimented the new beverage.

Without a sip, Abigail placed the chilled glass on a side table with a soft thud, a silent testament to her growing impatience. Her stomach flip-flopped as she reached her hand and placed it on Malik's upper thigh. Relieved he didn't push her hand away, she let her fingertips caress his lap in smooth, fluid motions.

"Abigail, I—" Malik started, but the words stuck in his throat. Unable to speak, Malik stilled Abigail's hand with his hand.

"Malik," she breathed, her voice a silken thread pulling him closer.

"Abigail," he began, his tone a mix of caution and yearning, "there are things about me. Important things you need to know before..."

"Shh, talk later," she interrupted, her hands moving from his lap to find the hem of his shirt with an impish determination.

Malik intercepted her path as she moved forward, his hands resting on her wrists with a tenderness that only spurred her. The fabric of his shirt rustled under her touch as she attempted to untuck it from his pants.

"Please, just listen—" he insisted, pulling so they were both standing.

A sudden burst of energy erupted into the room before another word could be whispered into the void. Malik's exuberant Labrador, Baxter, bounded in with all the grace of a freight train, his tail a relentless pendulum of excitement smacking furniture in his path.

"Whoa!" Abigail's foot caught on the dog's enthusiastic greeting, her balance tipping precariously. Her arms windmilled through the air, instinctively seeking anything to right herself in the unseeing world.

"Abigail!" Malik's voice was alarm-sharp, his detective instincts kicking as the scene unfolded.

Panic surged through her veins like liquid fire, each heartbeat a drumroll before the inevitable crash. But the fall never came. Instead, there was the solid presence of Malik, his arms encircling her waist, steadying the world once more.

"Got you," Malik whispered against her ear, his breath a

warm draft on her neck. The proximity was alarming, intimate, and far too stable for a man who should have been fumbling to find her in the dark expanse.

Her heart raced, a frantic symphony playing for an audience of two plus one canine interloper. The warmth of his body seeped through her clothes, grounding her at the moment, yet her mind was adrift, piecing together fragments of a puzzle she hadn't known existed.

"Sorry about that," Malik chuckled nervously, trying to lighten the mood while still holding her close. "Baxter has the grace of a baby rhinoceros but is young and built like a tank."

"I'll count myself lucky there was no horn." The quick reply did nothing to mask the tremble of her nerves, which still felt like her body was in flight. She could feel Malik's chest rise and fall with each breath, and the steady thrum of his heartbeat was a reminder that she was still suspended in his arms.

"Are you okay?" His hands ran along her body, assessing for damage before he helped her regain her footing and stand.

"Fine," she lied, unwilling to admit that her equilibrium had been shaken. "Just didn't expect a welcome committee."

"There's never a dull moment around here." While the words should have been jovial, they lacked sincerity. Since the fall, their conversation felt scripted. They each played their part, not deviating from the safe responses and avoiding the murky truth surrounding them. Something was bubbling to the surface, and it would not be pleasant.

Abigail remained acutely aware of his hold on her, the strength in his arms, and the questions bubbling beneath the surface. Oblivious to the human drama, Baxter nuzzled against her leg, a furry embodiment of innocence.

"Let me get you seated again," Malik said, guiding her back into her seat. "I'll put Baxter in the other room."

"No," Abigail said, stroking the dog's head. "He has settled, and I believe you had something to say." Baxter offered a buffer between herself and Malik, which she felt she needed. Abigail was also concerned that if Malik walked away now...would she be there when he returned? If she relied on her instinct and gut, she would walk away, just like she had with Levi.

Abigail could hear Malik's hands wringing and then rubbing against his thighs. The tension emanating from Malik sizzled in the air. Their tension no longer spoke of sensual pleasure; it choked on fear.

"Malik, how—" Abigail began, the words snagging like fabric on a jagged edge. The silence that followed felt gritty and grating. Her heartbeat sounded irregular, and a static churned in her mind. It felt like the silence that hung after her incomplete question was attacking.

"Reflexes," he said, answering the unasked question. "I just... reacted."

But Abigail's mind was a maelstrom of sensation and suspicion. She had lived a life devoid of visual cues and had experienced her fair share of falls. His grip on her had not been the accidental touch of arms flailing in a delayed reaction. This catch was deliberate and precise.

"Reacted?" she echoed, her laugh brittle. The sound felt out of place, a foreign object in the space between them.

"Like I said, Baxter is full of surprises." Malik's attempt at deflection was clumsy; their usual dance of witty banter was now a clumsy misstep.

"I see," Abigail said, settling back into her chair. She folded her hands in her lap, fortifying herself for what came next. And as she sat there, her heart a drumbeat of conflicting emotions, she knew that whatever came next would change everything. "Plausible. But not truthful. No more deception." She spoke in a staccato rhythm, each word a terse declaration that left no room for argument. She was done with the charade.

Malik shifted in the armchair, the creak of the leather betraying his discomfort.

"Abigail," Malik began, his voice a ghostly whisper, "there's something I have told no one."

Her impatience for a straightforward answer clawed at her insides. She held her mouth firm, straining to resist the urge to yell. Without answers, she didn't know what to yell at. She remained silent and unmoving, at the mercy of whatever Malik revealed.

"I was born... different," he continued. "I can see, Abigail."

The words fell like a guillotine, slicing through the quiet room. Her heart thudded painfully against her rib cage, a captive bird desperate for escape.

"Why?" The word escaped her, a solitary soldier charging into an ambush of confusion and betrayal.

"Why what?" Malik questioned back. "Why can I see? Why didn't I tell you? Why didn't I broadcast it to everyone? I don't know why I can see, but I didn't tell anyone because this world isn't kind to those who are different." The bitter taste of reality punctuated Malik's words.

Abigail's hands clenched into fists, nails digging crescents into her palms. She felt the sting of tears threatening to spill, a saline river eroding the banks of her composure.

"I never intended to get close to anyone. But I met you, and I could not walk away. As we stood in the Museum lobby, I knew I should, but I didn't. Being with you felt like the first time someone saw me."

"And yet, you have been seeing me all this time." Abigail shot back.

Malik let out a humorless gurgle, a sound that hovered between regret and resignation. "Yes, I've seen you—the courage in your smile, the resilience in your stride. But more than that, I've felt you. And that had nothing to do with my sight."

Her breath hitched, and she bit down on her lower lip, a feeble attempt to tether herself to the moment. How could she reconcile the man whose touch had offered such comfort to the new man now sitting across from her?

"Malik," she said, trembling, "you don't understand. For me, trust is hard. What you've done, rather your omission..." Her words trailed off, strangled by the swell of emotions that rose like a tide in her chest.

He moved then, a subtle lean forward, "I know you feel betrayed. But please, believe me, it was never about deceit. It was about survival."

"Survival," she repeated, tasting the bitterness on her tongue. "Couldn't any lie be justified as personal survival?"

"Abigail, I—" Malik started, but she raised a hand, a silent plea for space, time to think, and breathe.

"Please, just stop," she whispered. Her other senses rallied around her, constructing a mental image of him—of them—in this fractured moment.

"Malik," she said after a long silence, her voice steadier now, "I need to be alone. I need... I need to think things through for myself."

With those words, she rose from the couch, her every movement deliberate. Her world was forever altered by the revelation that the man she thought she knew had been a mirage.

The echo of Abigail's pronouncement still lingered in the air, a stark contrast to her earlier laughter that had warmed Malik's apartment. Her fingers grazed the back of the couch as she steadied herself, preparing to retreat into solitude. But Malik wasn't ready to relinquish his grip on the evening's unraveling narrative.

"Abigail, wait," he pleaded, his voice an odd cocktail of urgency and caution. He stepped toward her, arms half-raised, not to hold but to express his need for her to stay, like a wall. "There's something else I need to tell you."

She froze, mid-step away from him, her breath caught in an invisible snare. "More?" she asked, incredulity lacing her words like the biting edge of a winter chill. "What now, Malik? What other secrets have you been keeping?"

Malik exhaled slowly. "That night, at Club Ke Kino—I was there."

Already frozen, her inside felt like they crushed in on themselves. Her lungs forgot how to move, and her throat tightened. Abigail's voice was raw with physical pain as she sputtered a confused response. "You were... where?"

"Club Ke Kino. The night you went out with your friends. I was there. I was..."

An icy dread seeped into Abigail's veins, her thoughts racing and colliding like atoms in a furious reaction. "Is this your idea of some twisted game, Malik? Were you stalking me?" How had she not known that she had touched, tasted, and smelled so many people that night? It was a blur on her senses.

"No!" His denial was swift and emphatic. "It was by chance. I saw you and felt drawn to you even then. I didn't follow you; it was a coincidence."

"Coincidence," Abigail scoffed, the word dripping with skepticism. "How convenient for you." He had seen her and been drawn in. Did he watch her give in to the hands of strangers? Or had he..."Who were you? At the club, who were you?" she demanded.

"Please, Abigail, you know who I was—" Malik began, but she cut him off.

"Enough," she said, her voice cracking under the weight of her emotions. "I can't. I don't want to hear anymore. I need to leave."

"Let me walk you home," he offered, taking a tentative step closer. "It's late, and I—"

"I said enough!" Abigail's shout pierced the tense hush that had befallen the room. She turned away from him, her hands fumbling for the door handle, her thoughts a blur of betrayal and confusion.

"Abigail, please." His words were a whisper, lost in the space between them. "At least let me explain—"

"Save it," she interrupted, her tone resolute even as her heart pulsed erratically against her ribcage. "I don't want your explanations, excuses, or company. I'll find my way home."

With that, she pushed through the door, wanting to leave it all behind. But the cloud of chaotic thoughts passed through the door with her. The smell of rain wafted in from the open doorway, mingling with the turmoil that churned in the air.

"Abigail," he pleaded, the word barely above a gasp. "You can't understand what it would mean if people found out. It's not just about me—my life could be in actual danger."

"Malik," she said, her voice barely audible over the whir of the city outside. "I—I don't know what to say."

"Then say nothing to anyone else, please." His words were rushed, almost stumbling over each other in their haste to be heard. "This secret, it—it's bigger than us, Abigail. If my sight is exposed, my life as it is would be over."

Abigail's breath hitched, her fingers curling into fists at her sides as she grappled with the revelation. A vortex of thoughts and feelings collided inside her mind: anger, betrayal, fear. Yet beneath it all lay an inexplicable concern for the man before her.

"Say something," Malik urged, reaching out but stopping short of touching her.

She shivered, though she couldn't be sure whether it was from the chill of the night or the intensity of this moment. Her senses, usually so reliable, now seemed to swim in confusion, each grappling with the new reality Malik had thrust upon her.

"Is that why you've been hiding? Living half a life?" Her question hung between them like the mist that crept along the city streets, invisible yet palpable.

"Exactly. But there's more at stake than just me. I have cases and people who rely on me. My vision needs to remain...hidden."

Amidst the chaos of her emotions, Abigail's mind latched onto a single, unsettling thought. She considered his words, the weight of their implications sinking into her like quicksand. Could she carry this secret? It wasn't her secret to tell, but could she be trusted to remain silent?

"Malik, I..." she began, but the sentence dwindled into the sound of her heartbeat throbbing in her ears.

"Please," he whispered, the plea etched into every line of his tense form.

Silence fell, oppressive and thick. Abigail took a step back, her cane forgotten as she navigated by memory and raw instinct towards the exit. The door stood ajar, a gateway to the obsidian night beyond.

"Abigail," Malik called out again, but the clamor of her internal struggle, a cacophony of doubt and disbelief, drowned his voice out.

Without a word, she slipped through the door, the cool air embracing her as she stepped into the unknown. Behind her, the apartment remained, a tableau of unresolved tension and unanswered questions.

The last thing she heard as she walked away was Malik's AI's soft, mechanical voice, offering assistance with an oblivious cheerfulness bordering on mockery.

"Detective Callahan, would you like me to secure the premises?"

"Shut up," Malik muttered, his plea hanging futile in the void left by Abigail's departure.

Chapter 19

The key scraped off the lock, scarring the door's painted veneer. Exasperated, she asked Jules to unlock her apartment. The door swung open with such force that it rebounded when it hit the stopper and threw a hissy fit back at Abigail. Even lifeless objects seemed determined to mess with her this evening. She stepped inside. The air held the stagnant scent of an unoccupied space, an unused lemon cleaning agent still lingering from the morning's rush. Shutting out the world, she slammed the door behind her.

"Home sweet home," Abigail muttered as she felt her way across the room until her fingers carelessly brushed against something plush—the armrest of her ever-inviting couch. She crumpled on it in no time, allowing its cushions to absorb her weight and virtually envelop her in their customary soothing embrace. But today was different; comfort was a fleeting fantasy overshadowed by Malik's confession. A man who can see living among them.

Her phone buzzed into existence on the coffee table ahead, jolting Abigail out of her contemplative episode. By sheer practice over the years, her hands deftly reached for it, maneuvering through familiar territory based on memory. A tap followed a casual swipe, and Malik's voice poured out of the device, maintaining its warm undertone despite an underplayed desperation.

"Abigail...please," His words seemed to fill up space around instigating goosebumps along their path—as real as a physical caress could be minus actual contact. "You probably don't want to hear from me right now, but I want you to know—I am sorry. You are important to me, more than anyone I have ever met." Commanding simplicity coated every syllable. "There's so much left unsaid...call me as soon as possible?"

Abigail sunk deeper into the couch as her mind replayed his message, each syllable punctuated by the rhythmic ticking of the clock on the wall.

"Malik..." she murmured, imagining the contours of his face, which she'd traced with curious fingertips on their first date. His shape had been exhilarating, and every touch and taste explored a world she'd constructed from sound and scent. And yet, he withheld from her the one truth that painted his world in vivid colors she would never see.

Call me. Malik's plea echoed in her. To call or not to call was the question poised on the edge of her consciousness, teetering between the desire for understanding and the instinct to protect her vulnerable heart.

Abigail's heart thrummed between the urge to dial his number and the impulse to cast the phone aside. She tucked the phone into the couch cushion to ensure she did neither.

With another buzz, the phone demanded attention, but Abigail did not retrieve it; it didn't matter who the caller was; she was in no mood for conversation.

Catching on to Abigail's desire for alone time, Venus, in all her feline glory, let out a soft meow and sprung onto Abigail's lap, expecting the opposite. She nudged her head against Abigail's hand, desperately craving some petting. Contrary to expectations, Abigail swiftly withdrew her hand.

In a classic cat-like display of displeasure at her owner's lackluster response, Venus persisted and affectionately pressed herself into the warm comfort of Abigail's chest while sweeping her fluffy tail animatedly into Abigail's chin, a sensation that was impossible to ignore.

Contending defeat against the unstinted affection she was being showered with, a defeated groan escaped Abigail as she gave into stroking Venus' supple coat. Occasionally, scratching behind the ears amplified the bonding moment between them.

Before long, having been thoroughly appeased by attentive strokes and cuddles, Venus snuggled cozily onto Abigail's lap, forming a purred fur ball of contentment, proof enough she had secured victory in reclaiming attention from 'her person.'

The silence in Abigail Sorensen's apartment was tangible, wrapping around her like a shroud. "Jules," she started, her voice threading through the hush. "I need to talk." She moved Venus off her lap so she could begin pacing. The movement in the room helped to solidify her thoughts.

"Of course, Abigail." Jules' voice emanated from the speakers with a softness that belied his artificial origins. "I am here for you."

She hesitated, biting her lower lip. "It's about Malik... he has asked me to keep something significant, a secret. From everyone." Abigail felt the weight of the words settle between them, even if it was just with an AI.

"Do you not want to keep Detective Callahan's secret?" Jules inquired.

"I don't think the issue is about want. I am not sure if I can. Can he ask this of me? To be part of a lie?" Her question hung in the air, mingling with the faint hum of the climate control system.

"Legally, no. Ethically, it is subjective," Jules responded, his attempt at wisdom almost comical in its clinical precision.

"Ethics are more complicated when feelings are involved."

"Secrets have strained even the strongest bonds."

"Strain..." She paused, letting an idea form in her head. "Yes, but secrets also protect, don't they?" It was as though she were trying to convince herself, seeking validation from the one entity programmed never to judge her.

"Protect or imprison," Jules countered sagely. "It depends on the perspective."

Abigail stopped near the large window, the cool glass a stark reminder of the barrier between her inner turmoil and the world outside. "He says he cares for me," she mused aloud, her breath fogging the pane and drifting back to her. "If that's true, how can he burden me with such a risk?"

"Perhaps because he trusts you," Jules surmised. "Or perhaps because he has no other choice."

There was too much information bouncing around in Abigail's mind. Her assumptions about how the world operated came crashing down in just a few minutes. But how much of that was Malik versus the belief in sight?

"Jules," Abigail's voice broke through the quiet, "could you do something for me?"

"Of course, Abigail," Jules' smooth, gender-neutral timbre responded immediately, a hint of warmth programmed into its cadence. "What do you need?"

"Search the net. Look for any rumors or... confirmed cases of people with sight."

"Searching now," Jules affirmed. A series of soft clicks and beeps followed as Jules tapped into various data streams. Abigail pictured the AI sifting through digital noise, sorting fact from fiction with algorithmic precision.

"Presently, there are less than twenty unsubstantiated rumors concerning individuals who claim to possess sight globally," Jules said after pausing. "However, no credible evidence has confirmed such assertions."

Abigail nodded slowly, her heartbeat thudding against the stillness. She had expected as much, yet the uncertainty did nothing to ease the knot of apprehension coiled tight in her chest.

"Malik would be vulnerable if he were exposed," Abigail spoke, tasting the bitterness of the thought. "Not just his career... but his whole life could unravel."

"Abigail," Jules interjected gently, "it's important to remember that while sight may change perceptions, it does not alter the essence of a person."

"The essence of Malik is the same, but the whole dynamic will be different. He has an advantage," Abigail reflected. "I can't think about this any longer," she said, heading to the bedroom.

"I am too jittery to go to sleep. I'll bake." She changed directions mid-stride to go to the kitchen. With methodical precision, she began arranging her ingredients and baking materials. The dry ingredients were labeled in the pantry cupboard; she pulled out the ingredients and placed them in her preparation area.

Baking is one part science and one part passion. The measuring and proportions provided the science. Abigail relied on a food scale to measure her ingredients. "Scale, reset to zero," Abigail told the scale after placing a mixing bowl on the flat surface. "Scale, target 200 grams," she instructed before adding the sugar. Abigail paused for the updated reading, adding or removing a bit at a time to get the accurate amount. She continued this way for all of her weighted ingredients. Lost in measurements, her mind released some of the tension from earlier.

The preparation of the fresh ingredients was the passion. It offered meditative relaxation as her hands moved and her senses took in the fragrances. Abigail grabbed two lemons from the fridge and zested each with smooth precision. The first few passes were the most impactful, as the lemon rind released its essential oils. A citrus bouquet that reminded her of Malike, her mind returning to the painful thoughts.

Abigail finely chopped two sprigs of rosemary. The herbaceous scent mingled with the smell of lemon, creating a calming aura for Abigail's soul. Still a reminder of Malik, but muted with the addition of the herb.

When all the ingredients were combined and the dough put away in the fridge to work its magic, Abigail felt calm and ready for sleep.

"Tomorrow," she promised herself, clinging to the hope of clarity with the new day. "I'll figure it out tomorrow."

"Would you like me to play some soothing nocturnes?" Jules offered its voice a gentle nudge to direct her to a place of repose.

"Thanks, something low, maybe brown noise?" Abigail replied, brushing her fingertips along the textured surface of her duvet as she sat on the edge of her bed.

"Starting brown noise. Goodnight, Abigail. Call if you need anything," Jules said before the room fell into an expectant hush with only the low rumble like the sound of a distant waterfall.

She undressed methodically, the soft rustle of fabric against skin sounding unusually loud in the quiet. As she slid between the sheets, the crisp scent of lavender from her linen spray flirted briefly with her nostrils, offering a fleeting solace before dissipating into the shadows.

Lying there, Abigail's mind churned, replaying Malik's revelation in a loop. His voice, usually a smooth balm, now felt like a serrated edge scraping against her resolve. Each toss and turn of her body was a desperate search for a position in which her heart might settle, but it remained elusive, fluttering like a bird trapped in her ribcage.

As the night crept by, Abigail's thoughts swirled like leaves in an autumn wind, each gust of doubt sending them spiraling anew. She clutched her blanket tighter, seeking a mooring in the storm. But even in her quest for slumber's sanctuary, she knew some questions refused to be silenced by dreams.

Abigail's breath hitched, a thin strand of consciousness snagging on the jagged edge of a nightmare. The world behind her eyelids erupted in unseen terrors, each more vivid than the last. In this dreamscape, shadows morphed into the grotesque silhouette of her assailant from five years ago, a phantom stitched together by fear and memory.

"Can you feel it? The way I can see you squirm," the shadow hissed, its voice a serpentine slither that coiled around Abigail's heart. "Sight is power, and you... you're just stumbling in the dark."

She recoiled, the stench of musty sweat and malice filling her nostrils as if the specter were indeed there, looming over her vulnerable form. Her hands fumbled through the void, reaching for anything to anchor her to reality.

"Stop!" she cried, her voice cracking with terror. But the shadow only chuckled—a sound like shards of broken glass tumbling through the night.

"Powerless," it taunted, the word echoing in the hollows of her mind.

The cruelty of the words clawed at her, dragging her deeper into the abyss of her fears. A tear escaped, tracing a hot path down Abigail's cheek. She was caught in the web of her psyche, every thread vibrating with the echoes of the past.

"Malik," she whimpered, the name a feeble shield against the onslaught. Could his sight, too, become an instrument of control? He may be a good man at his core, but could his sight corrupt that? It already forced him to lie. The thought was a stinging slap, jolting her further awake.

"Get out of my head," she demanded of the darkness, but the battle waged on silently. Her fingers clenched the sheets, the fabric crumpling like the resolve she struggled to maintain.

"Please, just let me be," Abigail's voice broke, the plea spilling from her lips and dissipating into the heavy air of her bedroom. The imagined pressure of the shadow's gaze lifted, leaving her alone with the stark reality of her vulnerability. Should she call on Jules to comfort her? No, she would manage.

Abigail drew herself up with a shuddering inhale, wiping away the tears that had betrayed her stoicism. The crying felt cathartic and futile, like trying to cleanse only half of a wound that refused to heal. Sobs, which were half laughter and half despair, caused her chest to heave.

"Great, now I'm weeping in bed. What's next..."

She settled back against her pillow, the dampness a cold reminder of her ordeal. The room was silent save for her uneven breaths, each one a stuttering step towards composure. She focused on the steady rhythm, letting it lull her to sleep again.

"Okay, Abigail," she coached herself, "Just ride out the storm. Malik isn't him. Sight doesn't make the man."

But doubt was a persistent whisper, and as sleep reclaimed her.

Abigail's consciousness surfaced through layers of a murky half-sleep, the echo of her heartbeat loud in the quiet of predawn. She lay motionless, swaddled in bedsheets that clung to her skin, damp with the residue of nightmares. Each breath was a shallow draft as the surrounding air had thickened into a haze of uncertainty.

"Another round on the merry-go-round of torment, Jules?" she muttered into the darkness, her voice laced with self-deprecating humor that failed to mask the tremor beneath.

"Would you prefer a distraction, Abigail?" The AI's soothing and familiar voice flowed from the speakers like a balm. "Perhaps some light music or an audiobook?"

"Music," she decided after a moment's hesitation, seeking refuge in melody rather than words that might further open her thoughts.

As the first notes of a gentle piano piece cascaded into the room, Abigail rolled onto her back, pressing the heels of her hands against her eyes.

"Jules, can someone be inherently dangerous because they have something others don't?" She remembered Imani's explanation about private funding in research and power dynamics.

"Statistically?" Jules inquired, his tone neutral yet somehow aware of the gravity behind her question.

"Never mind." Abigail exhaled in frustration, sitting up and swinging her legs over the edge of the bed. Her feet found the cool floor, and she rose, navigating her way to the window by memory and touch. She opened it, letting the night breeze wash over her.

Jules continued, undeterred by her dismissal. "Danger is often a perception influenced by context and experience. But statistically, power imbalance can lead to misuse."

"Thanks, Jules. That's both comforting and utterly terrifying," Abigail said, sarcasm tinting her words as she leaned against the windowsill. The city's scents filtered in—a mix of exhaust fumes and the sickening scent of early-blooming flowers from the park below.

She padded back to bed, crawling under the covers once again. The weight of her thoughts was as oppressive as the darkness that enveloped her. The soft music still played, a stark contrast to the chaotic symphony in her head.

Abigail moved her hand only a few inches from her face. Wiggling her fingers, she willed her eyes to see. She had done this as a child, pretending to make out the shape of the form that was so familiar to her. Five digits were splaying out from a central oval, and she could see it in her head. She used to pretend the same with the house furniture. She knew the path and their form so well she could pretend that she saw it. But these were just fantasies of an imaginative child. The reality was she could not see by wishing for it. Malik did not have to imagine it. All he had to do was open his eyes.

Perhaps envy flecked across her emotions, not just fear and confusion. She could not say she had never wondered what sight would be like. Malik had something she did not, could not, possess. It hurt her early morning brain to consider all the implications.

"Let's just go back to sleep, Jules." Her voice was barely above a whisper, the edge of defeat fraying its borders.

"Of course, Abigail. Rest well," Jules responded, the finality in his tone signaling the end of their conversation.

Chapter 20

Abigail awoke to the rancid smell of stale coffee and the soft hum of the city outside her window. The digital clock on her nightstand announced the passing hours with a gentle, unobtrusive beep, marking the time since Malik Callahan's world-shattering truth had unfurled before her. She lay there, hidden in the fort of her bedspread, feeling every one of those beeps as if they were weights upon her chest.

"It's a new day, and I am just as confused as yesterday," she murmured, stretching her arms above her head.

She reached for her phone, its smooth surface familiar under her fingertips. The device vibrated with urgency as she swiped to unlock it, and the text-to-speech feature relayed the barrage of messages that Malik had sent. His words, synthetic and devoid of his warmth, buzzed around her like bees desperate to find their way back to the hive.

"Abigail, I need to explain. Please." Another message followed: "Abigail, please call." Weariness played in the last message like a final plea.

Abigail returned the phone to the table with an exaggerated thud. Her heart ached to forgive and make everything all right again. But that same heart bore the betrayal and didn't want to give in. Abigail felt her soul being torn in two. She did not like being the source of Malik's pain, but she was hurting as well. There were just too many thoughts racing through her head all at once.

If she could speak with Tessa or Imani, maybe she could work it out. Tessa would bring her passionate truth, and if Abigail wanted to call him every name under the sun, Tessa would help her find more insults. Imani would offer a level-headed point of view, not void of emotions, just more grounded and less name-calling. But no matter what happened, Abigail could never tell them the truth. She could never confide the source of her pain because the secret was not hers to share.

A wave of nausea surfaced. For the first time, she realized she would need to create her own lie. No matter what happened with Malik, she would have to deceive her friends. It was likely best to end her relationship with Malik now, before it could grow into something more. If it ended, the lie could be small, and there would be no fear of perpetuating it or accidentally letting it slip. It felt like a spiraling whirlpool sucking her down into the depths of confusion and heartache. She was going to drown in it.

A distraction to numb the pain was what she needed. Verbal banter with Jules could distract her. Abigail's sarcasm and Jules's flat retorts felt like a battle of nonsense, exactly what was called for to fight the turbulence in her head.

"Come on, Jules, give me some good news. Did my plant subscription arrive, or did the ferns get lost in the mail again?"

"Negative, Abigail. Your apartment remains a fern-free zone."

"I was very much looking forward to having a fern. Nilesh has Herbert. I believe he said something about a patient companion. I might replace you, Venus." Abigail taunted the unimpressed cat. Within seconds, Abigail's thoughts shifted. What if she was a bad cat mom? "Jules, are ferns toxic to cats?"

"My records indicate ferns are not considered toxic. Some felines even enjoy playing in their long leaves," Jules replied.

"Well, won't that be nice for her? They will probably gang up on me," Abigail complained.

"Abigail. If you require emotional support—"

"I require breakfast. That's what I require," she interrupted, standing up with resolve.

Abigail perched on the edge of her kitchen chair. Her fingers traced the rim of her coffee mug—there was no sugar today; she craved bitterness to match the churn of confusion within her.

"Jules, call in sick for me," she commanded, the words tasting like ash in her mouth. The AI hummed in response, dialing with efficiency Abigail once admired but now found cold, a reflection of the isolation wrapping around her like a shroud.

"Good morning, Fairwood High School. May I assist you?" chirped the chipper receptionist on the other end.

"Hello, Lydia. This is Jules on behalf of Abigail Sorensen. She won't be coming into work because of illness," Jules informed in its perfectly modulated tones.

"Feel better soon, Abigail!" Lydia's voice echoed a sentiment that seemed light-years away from being possible.

"Thank you," Abigail murmured, though she knew Lydia couldn't hear her gratitude or her sarcasm.

"Anything else, Abigail?" Jules asked, awaiting further instruction.

Sinking deeper into her chair as if it might swallow her whole and spare her from decision-making. "No visitors."

"Confirmed. No one shall pass unless you say otherwise," said Jules, taking on the solemnity of an ancient gatekeeper.

"Jules," she called out as if the AI had moved out of earshot. "Make a note."

"Ready when you are," Jules responded.

"Pro: He makes me feel alive. Con: He's also made me feel like a fool." Her voice cracked, betraying the turmoil beneath her stoic facade.

"Note saved," Jules said, the digital equivalent of a nod.

"Add another con for making me talk to myself," she added dryly.

"Would you prefer I talk back more?" Jules bantered.

"I believe you talk back plenty." Abigail deadpanned.

Jules called the school three more days while Abigail hid in the apartment fortress. While she knew it was self-indulgent to hide from the world, she couldn't imagine walking back into her old life without a resolution.

Tessa had left several messages and threatened to send the authorities to do a wellness check. Abigail returned a quick note to let her know it wasn't necessary. Had this been the longest they had gone without speaking in person? Even after the attack, Tessa was the rock beside her.

When a commanding knock vibrated the apartment door, Abigail assumed it was Tessa or the wellness check she had threatened. She was shocked when her mother greeted her at the door.

"Hello, my dear. Tessa let me know you were unwell. I stopped by with some soup to see how you were doing." Her mother's voice sounded caring and motherly. Gwen walked into the apartment, made her way to the kitchen, and deposited the soup. "Would you like me to make tea?" Her mother called back.

Abigail felt dumbfounded. Her mother was in her kitchen offering to make her tea. This had never happened before. "Yes, please," she called back and returned to her familiar seat on the couch.

Minutes later, Gwen joined Abigail and settled beside her

on the couch. Abigail felt her mother's fingers wrap around her hand. It had been years since she had held her hand like this. When had her mother's fingers become thin and her skin so rough? "Are you ill in the body or the heart?" Gwen asked.

Without warning, Abigail choked on the tears she had been holding back. "There-there," Gwen patted her daughter's hand. "It will be all right." They sat there in silence. Gwen comforted her daughter with pats and strokes. She didn't push for details or offer unsolicited advice. Gwen was just there and peaceful.

When Abigail had gained some composure, she apologized for the dramatic outburst of tears.

"No need to apologize, my dear. They needed to come out. Feel better?" she lovingly enquired.

"Yes, thank you, mom." Composed, Abigail could sip the tea her mother had left on the table next to her. The warmth felt good against her throat, raw from choking sobs.

"I am sorry," her mother whispered, as if barely holding back her own tears.

"Mom, you have nothing to apologize for. This wasn't your doing."

"I have plenty to apologize for. Unfortunately, as we get older, we see our past as a series of regrets. I am sorry for inviting Ryker to the anniversary party. It was wrong of me to push you into a relationship "

"Thank you." Abigail accepted the apology. "It means a lot that you said so. I am also sorry for losing my temper on such an important day." Silence fell between mother and daughter, each lost in their own thoughts. "You know, when you look back, you could focus on the happy memories, not the regrets." Abigail offered the sage advice to her mother.

"Oh, I do. Some regrets weigh heavy, that's all. You filled my life with so many happy memories. I hope the same for you." Her mother patted Abigail's knee with a feathery touch.

Abigail turned in her seat to embrace her mom. As she held her in her arms, she realized how thin she had become. She could feel her shoulder blades and ribs along her back. Abigail froze in the moment, accessing her mother's frail form. "Mom, what's wrong?" she asked.

"What do you mean, honey? Nothing is wrong." Gwen tried to dismiss her daughter's concern.

"Mom, I can feel it. You are so thin, and don't say you are losing weight. That isn't a healthy thin. What is wrong?" Abigail now demanded of her mother.

"Don't worry about it, my dear. We are taking care of you right now. Why don't you tell me what is going on with you?"

"Not happening. I am worried. I am becoming more worried with every passing second. Tell me what is going on."

"I am ill," Gwen finally relented.

"Ill, but getting better?" Abigail asked with a breath of hope, but intuition spoke otherwise.

"This isn't the type of illness a person gets better from." There was no sadness in her mother's words. It was regret, like the regret from earlier. "It is cancer."

"People fight cancer all the time and survive. First incidents of cancer have almost a 90% success rate for recovery now. Mom, why aren't you fighting?" Abigail pleaded to her mom, the tears welling in her eyes again.

"Oh, my poor dear. I fought. I fought the first, second, and the third time. But I have no more fight left in me for the fourth."

"You have had cancer three times before, and I never knew. How is that possible? Why didn't you say something, or Dad say something?"

"I didn't think I had to the first time. It was such a simple fix. I assumed the second would be just as easy. And by the third, I didn't know what to say. Another regret on a long list. Your Dad wanted to tell you, but I asked him not to. He reluctantly accepted my wishes. I now realize it would have been easier for him if he had your support. Regrets are worse than the cancer."

"Were you just going to die and say nothing?" Abigail felt anger boiling in her gut, merged with sadness and fear. It was a toxic combination.

"Watch your tone. I am still your mother. I don't know what I would have done. It is all a string of...regrets." Gwen paused, regaining her composure. "It is why I tried to rekindle your relationship with Ryker. I thought it would be easier on you if you had a partner."

Abigail snorted at her mother's plan. "You thought Ryker would make losing my mom somehow better?"

"Well, I see the absurdity of it now. After the scene at the party, I had a better understanding of your feelings towards Ryker." Gwen now huffed a genuine chuckle. "I was so stupid. What did you call him? A spineless jerk. Not the worst insult in the world, but you rarely insult people. It doesn't change that I wanted someone, aside from Tessa, in your life when I was gone."

They sat snug together on the couch. Emotionally closer in this moment than they had been in years.

"I did meet someone. Well, I met four someones, but only one I really like," Abigail admitted.

"And is this the someone that has you locked in your apartment stinking to high hell?" Gwen inquired, a little spark of the old judgy Gwen sneaking in.

"Maybe." Abigail huffed. She took a long breath and tried to reset. "He was great, and I cared for him. Maybe I could have felt even more. But now I don't know. Plus, I don't think I smell that bad."

"You can't smell yourself. You stink. Maybe you can't smell it over the stench of your kitchen filth. I don't think I have ever seen you leave that many dishes around. As for this man, the fact that you are taking it this hard means there is something in him you don't want to give up. I love your father dearly, but it wasn't always easy. How your grandmother hated me. She made the first few years of our relationship miserable." Gwen was lost in the memory. "She did everything she could to break us up. And your dad was a 'spineless jerk' as you phrased it. He never took my side. Broke my heart."

"What did you do?" Her mother had never spoken ill of Grama Sorensen.

"I was going to end it. But your grandmother fell down the stairs while your father was away. She was injured and vulnerable. I moved in and took care of her. It gave me a chance to know her better and vice versa. I spent a week with her. On the day your father was to return, I told her I loved her son, and he loved me. But if she didn't make room in her heart for me, it would be the last time I saw either of them. From that day onward, she referred to me as her daughter. I also talked with your dad about taking sides. Grama Sorensen would have had my back if your dad didn't side with me." Abigail was amazed at how much love her mom expressed for her dad and grandmother.

"So, are you saying I should push him down a flight of stairs and nurse him back to health?" Abigail teased.

"Hell no. One, I did not push her down the stairs, and two, it all comes down to being honest and accepting what happens. If it is meant to be, it will be." Gwen pulled her daughter close, wrapping an arm around her shoulders.

Abigail didn't recall when she fell asleep, but when she awoke she was curled up on the couch, the dishes were clean, a fresh pot of tea was in the carafe, and she was alone in her apartment.

Abigail finished baking the cookies from the dough, chilling in her fridge. It was an effortless task to pass the time. These were the same cookies she had shared with Malik at the cinema, the same recipe he had encouraged her to share with the world. He cared for her and wanted her to pursue her passions. He believed in her when she found it hard to believe in herself. Why could she not believe in him now? Was she just being selfish?

Abigail slipped off her kitchen chair and settled in the living room with her computer. " It can't be that hard to start a blog, right? " Hours later, she took the plunge and now had a site that broadcasted 'Coming Soon'. Her lemon and rosemary cookie recipe, written out with detailed instructions, awaited publication. It was hard denying the pleasure of clicking publish, but one day to think and reread with a rational mind would be best.

Abigail itched to call Malik and let him know.

"Abigail, it's Tessa again," came the crackling voice message, tinged with worry. "I know you're there. I've been calling all morning. Please, let me come over."

Abigail sighed, pressing her fingertips to her temples. Tessa's concern plucked strings of guilt and gratitude inside her.

"Listen, I'm coming over whether or not you like it," Tessa's voice continued, audacious as usual. "I'm bringing reinforcements—chocolate and that trashy sci-fi romance movie we love to hate."

Even through her turmoil, Abigail couldn't help but smile faintly. Tessa refused to be locked out of anything, least of all her best friend's life.

"Reinforcements accepted," Abigail mumbled, swinging her legs off the couch and brushing away the crumbs of solitude.

An hour later, the doorbell chimed, a sharp sound that Abigail usually welcomed. Today, it felt intrusive, mocking her frayed nerves.

"Coming!" Abigail called, her voice steadier than she felt. She navigated the familiar path to the door and flicked the lock open.

"It's about time!" Tessa marched in, arms laden with confectionery bliss and paperback melodrama. "You've been holed up in here for days. I can only imagine how terrible you smell."

"Maybe that's just your perfume. I'll have you know I don't smell." Abigail shot back, weakly attempting their usual banter.

"Ha-ha," Tessa replied flatly, clattering the items on the table. "Okay, talk to me. What's going on in that head of yours?"

Abigail's lips parted; the words tangled like yarn in her throat. "It's just... I miss him, Tess. His laugh, his..."

"But?" Tessa prodded gently.

"But he lied," Abigail's voice cracked. Unwilling to share more, for fear of having to lie or share Malik's secret,

"Abigail," Tessa said quietly after a while, "whatever you decide, I'm here. I know you are hurting, which tells me how much you cared for him. How about you tell your best friend what happened? It might make you feel better." Tessa's offer was genuine, but she could not understand the gravity of her suggestion.

"I can't do that. But it makes me feel better you are here," Abigail conceded.

She stood, navigating the room by memory and touch, every surface whispering echoes of the past days' isolation. She needed to make a choice. That much was clear. As she fingered the spines of books on the shelf, she realized each one held a story that ended. And so would hers, with or without Malik.

"All right, Tess," Abigail said, determination threading her voice. "Tell me more about this chocolate you've brought as a bribe."

"Only the finest from your favorite chocolatier," Tessa replied triumphantly.

Abigail sat alone, the remnants of Tessa's visit lingering like a comforted scent slowly fading. The remaining chocolate sat on the coffee table, its rich aroma a silent temptation to feed her emotions. Abigail's fingertips traced the embossed patterns on the foil wrap, contemplating the enigma that was Malik.

"Why am I so upset? Yes, it was a shock, but Malik didn't really deceive me. Well, he did by omission." She murmured to the empty room, her voice tinged with doubt and sadness.

She rose, pacing the confines of her living space. Her feet knew the steps by rote—the distance between the couch and the bookshelf, the bookshelf to the window. Every step should have been comforting in its familiarity, but today, they were a reminder of the walls closing in.

"Yes, Malik omitted the truth about his sight. But what was he going to do? Walk up and say he saw me dancing in a club a few nights ago. It is weird to say aloud. He saw me." She continued her pacing, trying to determine if there was ever a way this would not have ended, exactly as it had. Malik could have walked away, but would that have been fair to either of them? Was he supposed to be alone in life because of this difference?

A new anger was boiling to the surface, but not an anger towards Malik. Abigail was angry at a world that made Malik hide who he was; she was furious for his parents, who had to worry about their son's safety, and most of all, she was angry at herself for not even considering what toll this had taken on Malik.

"I am a selfish, self-centered idiot," Abigail reprimanded. "I have projected all of my fears into Malik's ability to see. Malik didn't set out to hurt me. I never even considered how much pain he has carried these years. He trusted me, and I ran off and ignored him. I have acted like an idiot."

"Yes, you have," Jules interjected.

"Um, I wasn't asking for a reply. But now that you have offered it, did you just come to this conclusion now or felt this way all along?"

"I don't feel anything, Abigail. But based on my observations, Detective Malik was justified in keeping personal information secure until sharing was required. If you had realized earlier, there would have been less moping."

"And why didn't you say anything earlier, oh wise one?"

"You didn't ask. Based on years of interactions, my algorithm indicated you would not be receptive to this information until you had reached the conclusion yourself."

"Well, in the future, tell your algorithm to keep its opinion to itself and kick me in the behind to smarten up. It could have saved us all a lot of time."

"I believe I understand the direction. I look forward to the verbal kick in the behind." Abigail wondered if Jules was making a joke at her expense. "Shall I assist in connecting you with the detective or drafting a note?"

"No, I need to get ready and head out," she replied, walking to the kitchen.

Chapter 21

Abigail's heart thrummed a staccato rhythm against her ribcage as she stood outside Malik's apartment door. One had grasped a box of cookies while the other reached for the door. The cold metallic surface of the door number beneath her fingertips confirmed she was in the right place. Nervousness played its jittery tune in her stomach, but determination kept her posture straight and pushed down the butterflies. She took a deep breath, inhaling the crisp taste of the rain that had already soaked her hair and shoes, having given up on the umbrella a few blocks ago.

"Okay, Abigail," she said, bouncing on her heels to energize herself, "this is it."

At her touch, the buzzer sounded its shrill note, slicing through the silence like a beacon. Footsteps approached from within, a confident cadence she had recognized as Malik's. The lock clicked, and the door swung open. She felt the wave of warmth emitting from the duplex apartment; it felt like sunshine in the miserable weather.

"Abigail!" His voice was rich with surprise and delight, wrapping around her like a pashmina shawl. "You're here! Come in, please."

"Um, Perhaps I should have called," the seeds of doubt sowing in her mind. What an awful sight she would make, soaked from the rain, likely leaving puddles in her wake. She had never had to worry about what she looked like. It was a strange sensation. Did her hair lie limp around her face? While her clothes were comfortable, at least they were before she got wet. Did they look good?

He reached out, and she felt the brush of his fingers against hers—a touch that sent a ripple of awareness through her—as he guided her inside and away from her spiraling thoughts. "Here, let me take your coat. There is no need to call. I am thankful I was here," Malik said eagerly, his voice tinged with hope.

"Thanks," she said, shrugging off the garment with care not to send the remaining rainwater everywhere. She passed the coat, hoping she didn't just drench him.

"How about I get a blanket and settle you on the couch? I can then help you remove your shoes and socks," Malik offered, guiding her further into the apartment.

"I can remove my shoes and socks," Abigail said defensively before adjusting her tone. "Thank you for offering to help. I would appreciate a blanket or towel to dry off and warm up."

"No problem, I can get you both."

Malik wrapped a blanket around her before settling her on the couch. He gave her a towel for her face and hair. Since she was snuggled into the blanket, Malik kneeled on the floor and removed the drenched shoes and socks. Without explanation, he left her alone in the living room.

A door opened, perhaps fifteen feet away, and she heard Malik say, "Calm, be good." Before she could ask if the instructions were for her, Baxter sat at her feet, his tail plunking happily on the floor.

"Baxter, scoot along for a minute." Malik returned to the floor, scooching the exuberant dog to take the spot at Abigail's feet. "I got you a pair of my thick socks to help warm up your feet, though I believe Baxter is eager to help as well." Malik raised her feet one at a time to slide the socks on.

"That was very nice of both of you." Abigail felt a zing of electricity from her feet to her heart at Malik's touch. As Malik returned to his feet, Baxter regained the position next to her legs.

"Can I get you something to drink?" Malik asked, already half-turned toward the kitchen.

"How about the chamomile tea?" she answered, pulling the blanket tighter.

"Coming right up," he said. Seconds later, she heard the rush of water filling a kettle and the clink of cups meeting the countertop.

Abigail breathed in deeply, letting the symphony of mundane sounds anchor her. She knew the next moments would chart the course of... something—potentially wonderful or disastrous. Only time would tell. But for now, she sat with her nerves and resolve, ready to face whatever came next.

"Here we are," Malik said, placing the cup in Abigail's hand. The heat of the cup transferred to her fingers, and the instant warmth was tingly and uncomfortable. She took a few sips and reached out to put the cup down until her hands and the cup acclimated.

"I brought you cookies, " Abigail said, pulling a small container from her lap. "They are Cherry Blossom and Green Tea Apology Cookies." She offered the box to Malik.

"You didn't need to do that or apologize." He opened the container. The sweet scent of cherries wafted out of it. "They smell...like spring." He took a bite of a cookie. "Oh, that is so good. Do you want one with your tea?" Malik reached out to Abigail to take a cookie as well.

After silent chewing, Abigail began, "I want you to know I have already made my decision about us."

Malik's breath hitched audibly. "You have?"

"Yes. But I still want to hear it, Malik. Your story. I also respect that my behavior may have changed your opinion of me. If you don't want to share, I understand."

"My feelings haven't changed. I don't think they could ever change," he said. His voice was steady, but she could almost feel him steeling himself for what would come. There was a shuffle of paws on the floor, and Baxter nudged her knee with his nose. Like a well-trained human, Abigail scratched his head and behind his ears, giving her listening attention a hundred percent to Malik.

"All right," Malik sighed. "I was born with sight, or rather, we assume I was born with it. The AI noticed when I was only a few months old. I found playthings faster than expected and had more of an attentive stare. My parents...struggled. They were scared. Scared of what it meant, scared of how the world would treat me."

Abigail tilted her head, curious. "Scared right from the beginning?"

"Yes, from the beginning," Malik confirmed. "It was unheard of. Their first concern was that someone would take me from them to study. But as I got older and could use the ability to help in the house, they realized that someone could use me, or, perhaps worse in their mind, I could learn to use it to my advantage. A cheat code to life."

She heard the wry smile in his voice, but there was an undertone of old pain, too. "They hid it," he continued. "Mom and Dad taught me to rely on my other senses to blend in. They feared that if anyone found out, I'd be ostracized, or worse. So, I learned to navigate the world just like everyone else without using my eyes. Creating the perception I could not see."

Abigail processed this revelation, picturing a young Malik experiencing the world in a way no one else had yet forbidden to share or explore that part of himself. How would she have fared if her parents had asked her to live without acknowledging sound? Becoming immune to every noise in fear a reaction could mean harm. It would be paralyzing.

That was Malik's reality.

"Does it bother you?" Malik asked, cutting into her reflection. "That I can see?"

"Bother me? No," Abigail said thoughtfully. "It would be a lie if I said I wasn't envious or perhaps more curious about the experience. But I don't resent you. It makes me wonder about all the things you see that I can't. How different our experiences of the world must be."

"Sometimes it's different," Malik conceded. "But like other experiences, it isn't as special if there is no one to share it with. I have seen some wonderful and terrible things but must keep quiet, as if I had seen nothing."

"It must have been lonely, carrying that secret." Abigail reached out, her fingers finding Baxter's soft fur. The dog leaned into her touch, a silent source of solace.

"Lonely doesn't begin to cover it," he admitted. And there it was, his raw truth, more revealing than any visual detail could ever be. The weight of it, a secret, must have weighed on him nearly every second of the day. She realizes if she was in his place, she would have probably hidden in her apartment, just like she has done these past years. Both had something they wanted to keep secret. Abigail had not been eager to share her story with Malik either.

"Thank you for trusting me with this," she said.

"Abigail Sorensen," Malik breathed out her name like a mantra, "you have this uncanny ability to make me feel seen, truly seen, even when I spend so much time hiding."

"I know a thing or two about hiding. It is a heavyweight

you have carried your whole life. I don't think you should carry this burden alone anymore."

"What are you saying?" Eagerness and hope crackled in his voice.

"Let me explain," Abigail interjected gently, turning her body toward where she sensed his presence. Her hands found his knees, grounding herself before continuing. "I've decided that whatever fears I have—fears about being hurt again or losing myself in someone else—they're not as strong as what I feel for you."

Malik absorbed her words, the silence stretching between heartbeats. The prickles of anxiety rippled under her skin. After years of being shut away, she felt parched for connection, and her gut churned with the fears that it could fail.

With each passing nanosecond without a response, the anxiety intensified. Unable to cope with the silence, Abigail continued. "Your story, your... condition," Abigail continued, choosing her words carefully, "doesn't change how I feel about you. It deepens it because you trusted me in a world where you can't trust anyone."

"Abigail," Malik murmured, his voice a low thrum that seemed to vibrate through her very core. "You're extraordinary. Do you know that?"

"I think you are extraordinary. I regret my initial response but don't want to live my life looking back at regrets." Abigail paused, reminded of her mother. If Abigail had not run off and locked herself in the apartment, her mom may never have come by. She may never have learned the truth, and that precious time on the couch curled into her mother would never have happened. "No, that is not the right. I don't regret running off. It gave me time to make sure I knew in my heart what I felt. I don't want to live with regrets and things unsaid. I love you, Malik Callahan." Abigail declared her epiphany.

"I love you too, with no regrets," he echoed, leaning forward so his breath brushed against her face for a gentle kiss.

"On to a more delicate subject." Abigail shifted in her seat, letting the blanket fall off her shoulders and pool around her torso. "What exactly transpired at Club Ke Kino?"

Malik gave a nervous laugh, not prepared to discuss that topic. "You must remember I didn't know who you were that evening," he squirmed in his seat. "I don't want you to think I am a creep. But since I avoid forming attachments, at least until I met you, I would go to the Club to connect, forming nothing real."

"So, we will call that efficiency instead of creepy. I get that." Abigail swallowed hard and, like a river gushed, spilled out the question on her mind. "I behaved with a certain expectation of anonymity. Even Tessa doesn't know everything that happened. Just tell me what you saw."

"Perhaps the question should be what I didn't see," Malik teased. "I will tell you everything, but first, promise you won't storm out of here and go back into hiding."

"I will do my best to remain open to communication. Also, Jules will see me running as an opportunity to call me on it and evoke a new skill set he has learned. Also, I have this new motto, 'no regrets'. I will try to remain in my seat."

"I saw you the moment you came into the club—the tentative touches with your friends, with your growing confidence reaching out to dance partners." Malik paused to take a sip of his drink and clear his throat. "We danced, we touched, and you licked me. I was in awe of you."

"Oh, my god. I licked someone's neck. That was you!" Heat radiated from her body as her head swirled with this new puzzle piece. Abigail felt both mortified and aroused at the thought. "I am not surprised you thought I would run. I am so embarrassed."

"No, don't be embarrassed. Your confidence was like a beacon attracting my attention." Malik let out a deep breath towards the ceiling. "I've already gone this far; I might as well finish."

"Oh, there is no chance you left the dance club immediately after I licked you?" Abigail half pleaded, half prayed. She pulled the blanket back around herself, trying to hide from what would come next.

"I followed you to the booth area..."

"You don't need to continue. I know very well what you saw next," an embarrassed Abigail interrupted.

"Maybe not so much what I saw versus what I did..." Malik let the last word trail off, waiting to see if Abigail, still hidden under a blanket, would interrupt again. With her silence, he continued, "Can I just say that I am very sorry you lost your bra on my account?" He skirted the specific details of their interaction.

A lone gasp escaped the mound under the blanket. Malik told the blanket monster on his couch, "Let me finish before I chicken out."

"There is more?" an exasperated voice squealed.

"Almost done." He tried to reassure, but it was pointless now. "I moved away from the booth when we...finished? But I kept watching you. You were in such a vulnerable state. I didn't want anyone to take advantage of it." Malik continued, his voice now exhausted and eager to finish his confession. "I followed you and your friend out of the club, at a distance, until you were out of the club district and what I assume was closer to home. I did not follow you all the way, just enough to make sure no one from the club, aside from me, had followed."

After Malik's last revelation, a hush fell between them. Malik was poised to stop Abigail if she made a sudden dash to the door. A moment later, a hysterical laugh erupted from under the blanket. The blankets slipped back down as she fell over on the couch in uncontrollable laughter.

"You are telling me that on our first blind date, I had previously groped and licked you. You had already half-undressed me, fondled my breast, and kissed me multiple times. God, that must have been awful for you." Abigail tried to push herself back up into a sitting position while wiping the laughter tears away. Malik reached out and helped her, since she was struggling with multitasking.

"I wouldn't say awful. It was physically uncomfortable. It took extreme willpower to resist picking up where I believed we left off."

Taking Malik's arm, Abigail pulled herself to his seat and sat on his lap. "This is not the story of how we met I would want to share with my parents. I guess it is not a story that we could ever share with anyone without the whole sight context. That isn't so bad. I don't think my self-confidence could handle it. We will need to continue writing our story and make sure there is parent-approved content."

"I have never felt like this for anyone. I can't imagine not being able to be with you."

Abigail smiled, noticing he said 'be with you' instead of 'see you', which was how she felt as well. "I want to explore everything with you, Malik—all the senses and experiences."

"Even taste?" Malik teased, a playful edge to his tone that made her heart flutter with anticipation.

"Especially taste," Abigail affirmed, her imagination already painting vivid strokes of flavor-filled moments yet to come.

"Then here's to new tastes," Malik declared with earnest. He guided her face to his, tracing light kisses along her jaw and neck. As their lips met, the intensity deepened.

Abigail's world ignited at the contact, her senses converging in a symphony of pure connection. His kiss was a cascade of flavors—bold and sweet like the darkest chocolate, thrilling her taste buds into a frenzy. She could hear the soft rustle of fabric as they drew closer, the gentle cadence of their breathing syncing in harmony. The warmth of Malik's body radiated against her skin, the sensation grounding her in the moment.

Their kiss deepened, a silent conversation where words were unnecessary. Abigail felt every ounce of her resolve melt away, replaced by a visceral need for closeness that only Malik could fulfill. Her hands found his face, fingertips tracing the contours that had become so familiar, even in the short time they'd known each other.

As they finally parted, Abigail escaped with a breathless chuckle, her cheeks flushed with the heat of their embrace. "You know, Detective, you might learn to be less reliant on those eyes of yours," she teased, her voice dancing with glee. "It's not all about what you see—it's about what you feel, hear, taste... and smell."

"Is that so?" Malik replied, amusement lacing his words as he tucked a stray lock of hair behind her ear. "Well then, Miss Sorensen, I am more than willing to be your pupil. Teach me to experience the world through Abigail's senses."

"Challenge accepted," she said, her tone light yet laden with promise. "But be warned, I'm a strict teacher."

"Good," he whispered, leaning in once more to brush his lips against hers in a featherlight caress. "I wouldn't have it any other way."

"Hmm, I wonder if blindfolds are still available, or perhaps we will improvise." Abigail could barely control her need to find out. "For now, would you like to reenact our first meeting? Refresh my memory on the details?"

"With pleasure. If I remember correctly, your clothing was damp that evening, too." Malik pulled her in close.

Chapter 22

The rain-scented breeze wafted through the half-open window, mingling with the aroma of fresh coffee that filled Abigail's quaint kitchen. She stood by the counter, her fingers tracing the braille on the sugar container as she listened to Malik's apprehensive voice, a subtle tremor betraying his usually unflappable demeanor.

"Abigail," Malik said, fidgeting with a tea cloth on the counter. "I feel bad about pulling you into my...I don't want to lie, but I do not have a full-truth lifestyle. I have pulled no one into my burden before."

She turned towards him, her blind eyes soft with empathy. "Malik, I understand, and neither you nor your sight are burdens. Your secret is safe with me," Abigail added firmly, her hand reaching out to find his. The warmth of his skin was reassuring, his pulse rhythmically tapping against her fingertips.

"Thank you," he breathed, his relief tangible in the air between them.

Abigail's internal monologue churned as she withdrew her hand and busied herself with pouring the coffee, the rich scent enveloping her. Her thoughts wandered to Tessa, her best friend since childhood, the one person who had been her confidant in all things. She would keep this from Tessa. Yet the weight of withholding such a significant secret from Tessa felt like a stone in her stomach.

She poured the steaming liquid with practiced precision, her mind a tumult of feelings. Her loyalty to Malik was fierce, and her protective instinct surprised her with its intensity. But Tessa—would she know a small wall would be raised around Abigail to protect Malik?

"Abigail, are you okay?" Malik's concern cut through her reverie.

"Of course," she downplayed her unease, the smile in her voice belying the tightness in her chest. "Just thinking about how best to navigate Tessa's lie-detector instincts."

The room echoed with sipping and the occasional clink of ceramic on wood. Abigail and Tessa's sisterhood already contained a vault of forbidden knowledge from years of wild fun. Abigail pondered and concluded that Tessa could be trusted to keep the secret, but there was no need to share it with her.

If anything, Abigail felt more concerned about Imani discovering the truth. Though she adored Imani and believed to have a deep understanding of her, Imani worked in a competitive field where Malik was the perfect match for research. Would Imani sacrifice one person for knowledge that could change millions?

"Let's not worry about the 'what ifs' today," Malik suggested, breaking into her contemplation. "Today, let's just be here together."

"Okay," Abigail agreed, her voice soft, still lost in thought. The pressure of keeping Malik's confidence warred against her bond with Tessa. It felt like she clutched onto two ends of a fraying rope, each strand threatening to snap under the strain.

Hours later, as Abigail was tidying the kitchen after some experimental cooking for her blog, Malik's voice broke through the silence. "Abigail, would you come over?" Malik's invitation crackled through the phone line like an unexpected spark. "There's something I want to talk about with you."

Her fingertips traced the texture on her apartment wall, a tactile map of her world. "That sounds ominous. Is anything wrong? Come over tonight?" she inquired, a flutter of curiosity dancing in her chest.

"Nothing is wrong, and tonight would be ideal. "Is it okay?" he inquired. Despite the pleasant words, the hairs on her arms stood at attention.

"Sure," she answered, though her heart thrummed against

her ribs, echoing her mind's unease.

As Abigail approached Malik's duplex later that evening, guided by the confident tap of her cane and Jules's murmuring in her earpiece, her senses were alight with anticipation. The sidewalk and pavement still radiated heat from the warm day. The street-level heat conflicted with the wind whipping around. She could hear the rustle of the tree leaves as the wind whipped through their canopies. Warm earth and upward winds spelled storm, as her granny would say. Abigail hoped it was only an environmental storm, not one waiting for at Malik's. Her fingers found the doorbell, the smooth surface cold and yielding under her touch. She pushed the button hesitantly, afraid of the next challenge.

"Come in, Abigail!" Tessa's voice greeted her from within. Surprise cut a sharp path through Abigail's thoughts as the door swept open.

"Te-Tessa?" Abigail stuttered, stepping into the warmth of Malik's home. The comforting familiarity of Tessa's obnoxious perfume enveloped her, but it did little to steady her racing heart. "What are you doing here?"

"Malik told us everything," Tessa bubbled, the excitement in her tone clashing with the heaviness settling in Abigail's stomach.

"Us?" Abigail's voice rose in pitch, a crescendo of confusion. That's when another layer of fragrance unfurled, one of cocoa butter and coconut—Imani.

"Tessa!" Imani's authoritative tone cut through the air. The rumble even stopped Abigail mid-step. "We agreed to let Malik explain." She chastised like a perpetually frustrated parent with an intolerable child.

"I couldn't help myself." Tessa must have been pouting, given the whine in her voice.

"How will you keep a secret if you can't help yourself? Tessa, a little self-control will not kill you." Imani flopped into a chair somewhere ahead of where Abigail still stood. She could hear Baxter moving in toward the now-sitting human.

"What secret? What do you know, and what the hell is going on?" The fear in each word grew in intensity as Abigail spoke. An unsettling fear perched in her stomach, threatening to constrict and convulse with each passing second.

"Abigail, I'm sorry," Malik's voice materialized from somewhere to her left, closer than she expected. His words seemed to float toward her, wrapped in the rich aroma of his aftershave and general Malik-scent. Her senses pulled her toward him instinctively.

"Sorry for what?" Abigail demanded, turning towards his voice, arms crossed. Her body language betrayed the tumult inside. "For inviting me here or for not trusting me enough to keep your secret? I presume that is what is going on."

"I'm sorry for everything, but mostly for how you were ambushed walking in the door." Malik took Abigail's elbow and directed her to what they now called her seat. As she settled, she could hear him shifting his weight, the creak of floorboards beneath.

"Tessa, Imani, if I could just have a minute without interruption to explain," Malik said, taking the armchair next to Abigail, the same one he had sat in to share his story only a few days ago. "Abigail, you are important to me, the most important person. I could not live with myself knowing I was making you lie to your most trusted friends."

"And what about my input in this decision? Did you not trust me to do what was right?" Abigail's throat constricted as she struggled to hold back the tears. Her hands tightened into fists as she willed anger to replace the hurt.

"Abi, it is because I trust you that I made this decision. You would have kept your word and said nothing. The pain will grow with each day that passed. You would have avoided your friends for fear of letting something slip. And one day, you would have resented me for pushing away your confidants." Malik rubbed Abigail's hands to loosen her fist and relax the tension. "We may not work, but I knew it was impossible with this hanging over you."

"You could have talked to me. We could have done this together." Abigail moused out the words. The hurt triumphed over the anger.

"In hindsight, that would have been a better option. I imagined it as a romantic gesture, a not control tactic. I am sorry."

Tessa, unable to contain herself any longer, exclaimed, "And now we all know, and it will be wonderful."

"Not exactly," Imani cut in without any of Tessa's happy exuberance. "Malik and I still need to come to an understanding."

"What do you want with Malik?" Within a nanosecond, her sadness was replaced by panic. Abigail turned her body instinctively, trying to put herself between Imani and Malik.

"It's okay, Abigail. Imani wants nothing from me. I am offering," Malik clarified.

"And I am declining," Imani interjected.

"Offering and declining what? Spit it out fast. I don't think my nerves can take much more of this," Abigail demanded.

"Malik is offering a secretive collaboration in my studies. I am declining his involvement." Imani explained. "I will not use friends to further my career."

"As I have already explained. The offer isn't for your career. You have good intentions. I may have biological data that could help not just explain the plague, but you would help me understand my situation. Potentially, others are living the same way I am," Malik pleaded his case. "Imani, if not for me or strangers. What if Abigail and I had a child? Wouldn't we want to understand?"

"A baby Abi or Malik, I call dibs on Godmother," Tessa exclaimed, not paying attention to the central theme of the argument between Malik and Imani.

Ignoring Tessa, Imani conceded, "Fine, but it is on my terms. If there is even an inkling of risk to you, I shut it down—without argument."

As Imani and Malik hashed out their agreement, Abigail stopped paying attention. Similar to Tessa, she lost interest when thinking about a baby. While they had only known each other for a few weeks, it felt like years, and Malik was talking about big future milestones. Abigail began daydreaming of bringing their two homes together. Would Venus and Baxter get along? They had already worked out who got which side of the bed, and as much as there was still much to figure out, Abigail wanted to jump to baby-making as soon as possible. She gave herself a shake to focus back on Malik and Imani as they reached their agreement.

"Let's have some drinks and toast to this crazy adventure," Tessa declared, ready to raise an invisible glass.

"Here, here," Abigail chimed in, a heaviness releasing from her body. Even if a storm were to rage outside, it was sunny and warm here. "I love all this comradery, but how did this all come to pass? I haven't made introductions yet."

"Well, you talk about your friends a lot. It wasn't difficult to find them." Malik explained. "I promise, I did not use any police resources to track them down. A friend who is also a teacher at your school and a famous scientist who shares another mutual friend. There was little challenge."

"Funny. That's not exactly what I meant. Did you message them and say you had a secret to share, so please come over and meet me for the first time?" Abigail clarified her asked.

"Not in those words, but in the general direction," Tessa confirmed. "It was more of a, before I mess up again, I need to talk to you both in person, type of message."

"Well, from now on, if there is a secret meeting to be had, I want an invitation."

"For sure. Our next secret meeting will include you." Malik assured, patting her hand like he was placating a child.

"I mean it. There will be extreme consequences if I am left out again. This is a team now."

Chapter 23

The bedroom's threshold loomed before Abigail and Malik like the starting line of an uncharted race, their footsteps syncing in a rhythm that vibrated with the thrum of shared anticipation.

"Are you sure you want to do this?" Abigail's voice was a whisper woven with excitement and the faintest trace of her usual shyness.

"Absolutely," Malik replied, his confidence filling the room like a song only she could hear. "Lead the way."

Abigail extended her hand, fingertips brushing against his palm before intertwining their fingers. She guided him to the center of the room with the ease of someone who had memorized every inch of her space.

Reaching the dresser, her hands skimmed its polished surface until they closed around the silk scarf she had placed there earlier. A river of fabric that would find a new purpose today. Turning back to Malik, she felt a smile tug at her lips. "This is going to be fun, Detective. I'm about to steal one of your senses; consider it payback for the secrets you kept."

"Fair enough, Miss Sorensen," he said, the corners of his eyes crinkling in delight. "Do your worst."

Abigail draped the scarf over his eyes, her fingers careful not to snag on his hair. He stood statue-still as she tied it, the knot resting with assurance at the back of his head. His breath hitched ever so slightly.

"Too tight?" she asked, even though her sense of touch told her it was right.

"Perfect," he assured her, a grin audible in his voice. "I'm all yours."

She couldn't help the flutter in her stomach at his words. The sensation of guiding him, of being empowered, brought an unexpected intimacy to the moment.

"Good." Abigail allowed herself a small, victorious chuckle. "You do not know how much I've been looking forward to this."

As she stepped closer to him, Malik swayed toward her warmth, as if drawn by her scent. She bit her lip in anticipation, knowing the intimacy they would share. This was more than an experiment; it was a challenge, an act of trust. As she reached out to touch his face, Abigail realized they were both venturing into the unknown, discovering new territories together today.

"Keep still," Abigail whispered, her fingers hovering mere inches from his skin. Her fingers made contact—a feathery stroke against his forehead, down the arch of his brow.

Malik remained still, as instructed. His usual quick-fire retorts were lost in the sensation of Abigail's fingertips tracing the bridge of his nose, skating over his shielded eyelids.

"Your face is so expressive," she murmured, her tone imbued with genuine curiosity. "I can feel the history of your smile and frown lines... They're all etched here."

"Never thought my face would be under such scrutiny," he joked, but the laughter didn't quite reach his lips, which parted as Abigail's fingers descended to trace their shape. The tickling sensation sent an involuntary shiver through him, which seemed to ripple back to her through the charged air between them.

A tremor danced down Malik's spine as Abigail's fingers left his lips, trailing a path into uncharted territories. The air seemed to tingle with electricity, charged by his heightened awareness in the absence of sight.

"Your body is quite the conversationalist," Abigail mused, her fingertips skating across the sensitive skin of his neck. "It speaks a language all its own."

Malik chuckled, a low and throaty sound. "Does it now? And what's it saying?"

"Curiosity," she replied, feeling the warmth that radiated from him. "A dash of anticipation... mixed with a hint of impatience."

"Guilty as charged," he admitted, relishing how her touch seemed amplified, each whisper of contact sending currents through his consciousness.

Abigail's fingers danced across Malik's collarbone. "Do you remember the museum? When your fingers followed a similar path across my collarbone? How I itched for you to explore more. I regretted not wearing a top with more skin exposure."

"Abigail," Malik moaned softly, the word slipping out like a secret he couldn't keep. His heart thrummed rapidly, a rhythm set to the tempo of her caresses.

"Shh," she hushed him gently, her hands now an ensemble of sensation as they coasted lower. "Focus on what you feel, not what you want to say."

She could hear the labor of his breath, the fabric of his shirt whispering in time with the rise and fall of his chest. It was more intoxicating than any confession, and she soaked it in, committing the cadence to memory. Her fingertips were instruments of discovery, each sweep over his skin like a paintbrush crafting a masterpiece.

Leaving a hand on his chest, she moved to stand behind him with an arm wrapped around his torso. She leaned her head and chest into his back, enjoying the sense of belonging and fit they experienced. With agile hands, Abigail removed his shirt and then her own.

Her fingers and palms traced the muscles along his arms, torso, and back. She felt the eruption of goosebumps across his skin. Despite the heat, he shivered. Abigail felt pressure behind her eyes as a well of tears threatened to pour—tears of pure happiness wrapped in safety. Each moment they touched, Malik's trust helped drive away the shadows of fear and doubt that lingered in her mind.

Pushing back tears that would only alarm Malik, Abigail focused on the sensation at the tips of her fingers. Enjoying that feeling, she let her lips follow the same path. With the softest touches she could manage, she traced feather-light kisses along his back and shoulders. Malik's body tensed; moving her hands down his arms, Abigail discovered his hands fisted in restraint.

"Should I stop?" Abigail teased, leaning in closer so more of her touched his back and nipped at his shoulder.

"No." Malik struggled to speak a single word, restraint consuming most of his energy.

Abigail returned and took his hand to lead him to her bed. Climbing up on the bed, she settled on her knees so they were nearly face-to-face with Malik still standing. "Well, you have been very patient with me. I think it is only fair I give you the same opportunity to learn with your hands." Malik groaned as he raised his hands to touch her skin.

At first, his hands were tentative and clumsy, but Abigail placed a hand over his to help direct. First, she moved his hand to trace her collarbone. Knowing Malik likely wanted to push his hand downward. She edged his hand up to cup her face. With her guidance, he explored the features of her face. His fingers were rewarded with small kisses whenever he glided across her lips.

Abigail reveled in the sound that escaped him - a soft, low chuckle as his fingers mapped the contours of her face. Her name fell from his lips, cherished and savored. She allowed herself a moment to indulge in the warmth that flooded her at the tender sound of it.

Emboldened, Malik let his hands wander more freely, tracing the curve of her shoulder, making her catch her breath with a bold sweep down her arm. His rough hands were like an artist's tools on her skin, drawing invisible lines and shapes only they could understand.

She gasped as Malik's hand reached her waist, his long fingers doing a slow dance over her sensitive skin. His touch was exploratory but careful, as though he was handling something precious. She felt another rush of emotions threatening to spill over, but held them in check.

"This is different," Malik murmured into the quiet space between them. "This feels...real."

"Real," Abigail echoed, the word settling and blossoming in their shared space. She felt her heart dance wildly as he continued his exploration, leaving her skin tingling in the gentle wake of his touch.

For a moment, they remained silent, their connection threading through each shared breath and the symphony of heartbeats echoing in unison. His hands moved purposefully, slow, across her bare skin, each second carrying a weight of unsaid words and unearthed feelings.

Abigail shivered as she felt Malik's gentle hand cup her face, his thumb tracing the path of a non-existent tear down her cheek. The tender and sweet touch almost brought her to tears again. She couldn't help but lean into his palm, her breath catching in her throat. His other hand trailed along her jawline, down her neck and collarbone, until it rested on her shoulder, feeling the rise and fall of her breath. Malik's warm fingers played with the fabric of her bra strap before sliding it down. She felt him hesitate for a moment before he brushed his lips against her skin, tasting her innocently in the room's silence. It was an intimate gesture that made Abigail's belly ache for more.

His fingers traced the outer edge of her bra, teasing to break the clasp that held her breasts back. Instead, he lowered his mouth. A small nipple buried in lace brushed against his lips, making him groan into it as he suckled gently, teasing it with gentle kisses and flicks of his tongue. Malik moved slowly, as if there was all the time in the world. One breast and then the other receiving the same attention. Satisfied with his teasing, he left her breast and refocused on Abigail's mouth.

As their lips met, his lips were warm and soft, like cinnamon and meringues. His stubble felt rough against her smooth skin, and she couldn't help but smile into the kiss; it was a different intimacy than usual. Her tongue traced the seam of his lips, and he let her in, opening up to her exploration. Their tongues danced together, tasting each other's secrets and curiosities. She could feel his hands wandering, tracing every dip and curve of her back, lingering on the small of her back before sliding up to cup her breast through the thin, lacey fabric. The warmth of his palm against her nipple sent shivers down her spine as he rolled it between his fingers, massaging.

"Are you sure you are not peeking?" Abigail needed to ensure their game remained fair.

"Not a bit. But I think you may be peaking," Malik said while giving her nipple a quick pinch to emphasize his play on words as he caught her mouth in a kiss.

Abigail ran her fingers through his hair, delighting in its coarse texture. She leaned into him more, feeling his muscular arms wrap around her waist as if holding on for dear life. Their hips ground together in perfect rhythm with their kisses and gasps for air. Their tongues teased as they explored every nook and cranny, tasting each other like new adventures waiting to be discovered.

Breaking away from the kiss, Malik trailed hot nips along her jawline before nibbling on her earlobe. He groaned when she grabbed his hair in response, urging him closer.

The bed springs creaked under their fervent movements as he rolled onto his back, pulling Abigail on top of him. The taste of sunlight lingered on his skin as her lips trailed over his neck, then down to trace the lines on his chest with a whisper of a touch. He let out a low groan at this newfound pleasure—the light brush of her breath sending shivers down his spine. She left a trail of tiny love bites and soft kisses along his ribcage, each one sending shockwaves of excitement through him. His heartbeat thundered against her ear in response, its tempo echoing through the room's silence.

Abigail pulled away to tease him with gentle bites on his earlobe before a husky whispered against it, "Do you like that?"

His response was interrupted by the frantic leaping of a cat across the bed, followed by an excited dog. Malik flipped himself up to secure Abigail so she wouldn't be tossed off the bed by the playful animals. 'Are you okay?" He asked, ripping off the blindfold and running his hands along her body, searching for injuries.

"I am fine. A little discombobulated from the jostling, but unharmed." She reassured.

"I should have left Baxter at my place, sorry," Malik grumbled with a frustrated apology.

"No, you couldn't. Not if you were going to spend the night. It might have been easier for me to come to you. Venus can be left alone one night. However, she would make me suffer later from being ignored."

"We need to learn to close the bedroom door." Malik shifted to usher the playing pets out of the room. He closed the door behind him.

"At least they are getting along. I heard nothing that suggested a fight or pain."

"Oh, they have become quick comrades. We should be more worried about them ganging up on us. As just illustrated. Now, where were we?" Malik slipped back into the bed, scooping her back into his arms.

Epilogue

Five Years Later

Morning light filtered through the sensor-activated blinds, casting a soft glow that roused Abigail from her slumber. The smell of brewing coffee tickled her nose, a signal that Malik was already. The energizing aroma drew her out of bed. Abigail tiptoed to the kitchen. "Good morning, my love," Abigail said, leaning in to embrace.

Malik padded his heart, feigning mocked shock, "Your stealth skills are improving. You might have had me this time if it wasn't for the sound of the bedroom door." Malik kissed the tip of Abigail's nose.

"I put you out a cup of tea. However, it seems Venus has developed a taste for chamomile tea." He nodded towards where their feline companion sat, licking her lips with an air of entitlement next to the steaming mug on the counter.

"Only the finest for our discerning lady. I am craving cranberry juice, ice cold cranberry juice this morning,"

"Let me help you navigate the minefields of toy block to the living room, and then I can bring you the juice and breakfast." Malik wrapped an arm around Abigail and took her hand in his.

Malik directed Abigail to the crescent couch, sweeping toy blocks and other hazards out of the way. He lowered her into the seat and securely tucked a blanket around her lap. "Malik, I am not ill or a three-year-old."

"I'm just making my wife extra comfortable. Be back in a few minutes." Malik hurried away, but not before giving Rosemary a gentle pat on the top of her head.

Rosemary stormed to Abigail s lap, embracing her lower legs in a powerful toddler hug. "Mama! Morning. Story?" the exuberant child demanded.

Raising her daughter to her lap, Abigail cuddled her in close. "How about a cuddle now, and I convince your daddy to play airplane with you when he returns?"

"Airplane!" The little girl's arms jutted out in both directions, and she took off to fly around the room. Her daughter's squeals of laughter created bubbles of joy in Abigail's chest.

Malik returned shortly, settling an overloaded breakfast tray over Abigail's lap. Before Abigail could comment, he explained, "Just making sure you have an option."

"Appreciate it. I hope you will forgive me, but I bartered with our daughter, and you are now in airplane servitude."

"AIRPLANE!" Rosemary squealed.

"Jules," Abigail called out, "I think it's time to change our auditory landscape. How about 'The Galactic Giggles' for our little pilot?"

"Switching to 'The Galactic Giggles,' "Jules replied in its smooth, modulated tone. A playful melody infused with electronic beeps and boops filled the room, simulating a whimsical space adventure.

Abigail listened to her daughter and husband's laughter while devouring the food tray. Abigail knew Malik was being kind when he said the tray held options. He knew she would consume it all, as she was ravenous at this stage of her pregnancy.

Abigail shifted the tray to one side. She stroked her belly, feeling the gentle kicks against her palm, each tiny movement sparking wonder. She imagined the baby, cozy in its world, unknowing of the vibrant life that awaited outside.

Malik and Rosemary had moved on to a cutthroat game of 'I got your nose,' in which Venus had also lost her nose to Rosemary's quick fingers. "I'll give you back your nose if you return mine and Venus'. You know she needs her nose," Malik asked his intelligent offspring.

"Daddy, I don't really have Venus' nose," Rosemary said, opening her hands wide for her dad to see.

"Had me fooled." Malik seamlessly moved into the following playful diversion. "Tickle monster is coming for you!" Malik warned, his voice a playful growl, and Rosemary erupted into high-pitched giggles as his fingers danced expertly along her sides, knowing where she was most ticklish.

"Daddy, no tickles!" she gasped between laughs, squirming with delight beneath his touch. Each time Malik eased up, Rosemary demanded, "More tickles, Daddy."

"Promise me you'll never get too big for cuddles," his hand mid-air poised for more tickles, depending on her response.

"Never!" Rosemary declared, with the earnestness that only a child could possess, her tiny arms trying to encircle him completely.

"Good," he replied, a contented sigh escaping him. "Because Daddy needs them just as much as you do. Daddy also needs a break. How about we make cookies for Aunty Tess and Aunty Imani's visit?" Rosemary's only response was darting off to the kitchen. Malik lightly kissed Abigail and grabbed the tray before he was off in pursuit.

Abigail scooted herself to the end of the couch and pulled her knitting basket up on her lap.

"Shall I adjust the music to 'Cozy Cottage', or would you prefer to continue listening to 'The Galactic Giggles'?" Jules proactively asked.

'Cozy Cottage' will work perfectly for this knitting. "I have progressed little since Tess and Imani were here last week for knitting club." Abigail picked up her work to resume as Venus assumed her spot next to her. Abigail's head bopped a few times before settling into her knitting nap.

When Abigail awoke, the house smelled like her now world-famous lemon and rosemary cookies, the first recipe she published on her website. Malik was seated over, with Baxter curled up at his feet. "Where's Rosemary?" Abigail asked, not hearing her normal buzz.

"Napping like Mommy. She played hard this morning."

"Mommy doesn't have 'playing' as an excuse." Abigail laughed.

"Mommy doesn't need an excuse." Malik reminded, for the umpteenth time.

They sat in silence, enjoying the reprieve of the chaos. Abigail absently caressed her outstretched belly; it would only be about three more weeks before they welcomed the new baby into their home.

She recalled when Rosemary had made her entrance into the world. She hadn't known it was possible to love something so much. The love she felt helped in a decision that had plagued them for a couple of weeks. Since her mother had been moved into hospice care, they weren't sure if they would bring the baby into that environment. Abigail wanted her mother to meet the baby, but her mother was rarely lucid and didn't want to cause undue stress in her final days.

But Abigail couldn't imagine not sharing this moment with her mother.

When they arrived in her mother's room, her father was already there. They propped her up with so many pillows that it was easy to rest Rosemary in her grandmother's arms. Gwen lovingly stroked Rosemary's arm, cooing at the newborn. "She is beautiful," Gwen said.

"She is," Abigail's father agreed, having yet to hold Rosemary himself.

Abigail cried, leaving her mother's room. She blamed it on

hormones, which was only partially true. She was so happy for Rosemary, that her mother had met her granddaughter, and that she had repaired her relationship with her mother. But her heart ached that it would likely be the only time. Her mother would never know that her granddaughter had looked up and at least see what babies see.

Abigail said, "I wonder if he will have eyes like his Daddy and Big Sister?"

"It doesn't matter in this family," Malik replied.

Abigail's Culinary Classroom

Welcome to my sweet corner of the internet, where flour-dusted hands and the aroma of freshly baked cookies will awaken the senses. I'm Abigail, a devoted biology teacher, and in the midst of shaping young minds, I've discovered my own form of artistic expression in the kitchen.

Today, I'm delighted to share a recipe encapsulating my love for vibrant flavors: Lemon and Rosemary Melt Cookies. Picture this: the zesty burst of lemon dancing harmoniously with the earthy, fresh rosemary notes and a sweet sugar dusting.

So, grab your apron, preheat that oven, and embark on a journey of taste and tradition. Prepare to infuse your kitchen with the aromatic symphony of citrusy zest and herbal allure as we bake our way to a moment of pure bliss.

Ingredients:

- 1 cup (226g) butter, softened
- 1 cup (200g) granulated sugar
- 1 large egg, room temperature
- Zest of 2 lemons
- 1 tbsp of fresh lemon juice
- 2 tsp, finely chopped fresh rosemary, about 2 sprigs
- 2 cups (240g) all-purpose flour
- 1/2 cup (80g) cornstarch
- 1/2 tsp salt
- Powdered sugar for dusting

Instructions:

Cream Butter and Sugar: In a large mixing bowl, cream the softened butter and granulated sugar until combined. A fork or electric mixer will work.

Incorporate Wet Ingredients: Add the egg, lemon zest, lemon juice, and chopped rosemary to the butter-sugar mixture. Blend until well combined.

Dry Ingredients: In a separate bowl, whisk together the all-purpose flour, cornstarch, and salt. Gradually add the dry ingredients to the wet, mixing until just combined. Do not over mix.

Chill the Dough: Cover the cookie dough and chill it in the refrigerator for at least 1 hour. This helps blend the flavors, make the dough easier to handle, and avoid spreading when cooking.

Preheat Oven: Preheat the oven to 375°F (190°C). Line 2 baking sheets with parchment paper.

Form Cookies: Take a 1/2 tablespoon-sized portion of chilled dough and roll it into balls using your hands. Place half of the mixture on one baking sheet. Return the remaining dough balls to the refrigerator.

Reduce Heat & Cook: Reduce the heat to 350°F (175°C) and bake the cookies for 13-15 minutes or until the edges are lightly golden. The centers may seem slightly undercooked but will firm up as they cool.

Cooling and Next Batch: Remove the cookies from the oven and let them cool on the tray for 5 minutes. At the same time, increase the oven temperature to 375°F (190°C). Prepare the next batch of cookies on the second room-temperature baking sheet. Repeat step 7, "Reduce Heat & Cook," for the second batch.

Cool on Wire Rack: After the 5-minute cooling period, remove the cookie from the sheet and place it on a wire rack to cool completely.

Dusting: Once the cookies are cooled, dust them lightly with powdered sugar.

Storage: To maintain freshness, store the cookies in an airtight container for 2 days on the counter and 1 week in the refrigerator. They can also be frozen for more extended storage (3 months).

Tips and Troubleshooting:

Ensure that the butter is softened but not melted for the right texture.

Use fresh rosemary for the best flavor. Chop it finely to distribute the flavors evenly before.

Chilling the dough helps prevent excessive spreading during baking, resulting in a more tender cookie. If your cookies are still spreading, try placing the dough balls in the freezer for 30 minutes before baking.

Do not over-mix the dough. Most of the unincorporated flour mixture will settle on the bottom; ensure this is scooped evenly before being incorporated into the dough early to avoid the need to continue mixing.

Why preheat to 375°F (190°C) and then reduce? Opening the oven door releases a lot of heat, so your oven needs to put energy into reheating. This provides inconsistent heat. Overheating the oven and then reducing the heat allows the oven to remain around the 350°F (175°C) target. For this reason, avoid opening the oven door during the bake.

For the best results, use the weights provided for the ingredients. The scoop and level method would work with this recipe if using cups.

Discussion Guide for Book Clubs

Please note that the following discussion guide contains spoilers for *Unseen Senses.*

I: Each character has a unique relationship with AI. Abigail and Jules appear to have a mutual dependency. Tessa and Riley have an antagonistic relationship. Imani believes she could love her AI, and finally, Malik shows resentment that AI would receive the lead detective credit in solving a case.

- What is your current relationship with AI?
- As AI continues to evolve, how do you see it being part of our day-to-day existence?
- What barriers would you hope AI could help humans overcome?

II: Abigail is unwilling to forgive Nilesh's deceit on their blind date, but she forgives Malik for hiding his sight.

- How do you compare the two falsehoods?
- Should Abigail have given Nilesh a second chance? Would you?

III: Abigail ends her date with Levi early because his singing voice hurts her ears. Abigail justified the ending of the date because the music was essential to Levi, and she didn't think she could be truthful about her opinion.

- Would you consider this a selfish or selfless act by Abigail?

IV: This novel's central theme was the imbalance of power, its abuse, and the fear it could generate.

- Did the fictional situation allow you to consider the imbalance from another point of view?
- Of these characters: Abigail, Malik, Tessa, Imani, and Jules. Who do you think has the most power to influence others?

V: For the purpose of exploring the other senses the author created a fictious world without sight. There were no physical descriptions of characters beyond what could be touched.

- How did you envision characters?

- Were the other senses sufficient to build the fictious world for the characters?

www.ingramcontent.com/pod-product-compliance
Lightning Source LLC
LaVergne TN
LVHW012044160826
845678LV00014B/2698